APR 1 5 2010   <u>Date Due</u>   **W9-AYP-593**

JUL ~ 1 2010

AN AVALON HISTORICAL ROMANCE

ROSE'S HOPE
Sandra Wilkins

When Rose Dennis begins her first job at B & B Mercantile in the winter of 1906, she befriends a handsome widower, Owen Emerson, his baby, Hope, and a dashing man named Richard Dobbs. Both men recently moved to Shawnee in Oklahoma Territory, and she is drawn to each of them.

Circumstances change and Rose takes care of Hope full time. She soon loves the little baby, but she hesitates to have any feelings for Owen because he seems to be in deep mourning. Richard, on the other hand, is accommodating in every way and seems almost too good to be true.

Which man loves her? Which man will only betray her? Her good friends, Ada and Gwen, try to help her make this important decision, but Rose knows only she can be the one to resolve her dilemma. With which man should she put all of her hopes and dreams?

Other books by Sandra Wilkins:

The *Heartland Romance* series:

Ada's Heart

ROSE'S HOPE

•

Sandra Wilkins

AVALON BOOKS
NEW YORK

Published by Thomas Bouregy & Co., Inc.
160 Madison Avenue, New York, NY 10016

Library of Congress Cataloging-in-Publication Data

Wilkins, Sandra.
  Rose's hope / Sandra Wilkins.
      p. cm.
  ISBN 978-0-8034-7757-5 (hardcover : acid-free paper)
1. Triangles (Interpersonal relations)—Fiction.   2. Shawnee
(Okla.)—Fiction.   I. Title.
  PS3623.I5485R67 2010
  813'.6—dc22

                                                    2009045272

PRINTED IN THE UNITED STATES OF AMERICA
ON ACID-FREE PAPER
BY HADDON CRAFTSMEN, BLOOMSBURG, PENNSYLVANIA

This book is dedicated to my grandparents—
Wilfrid and Louise Marak and Melvin and
Vera Broudrick—and to my great-grandparents
who shared their strength, love of music, humor,
moral values and pioneering spirit.

I would like to thank the following people:

The staff at the Santa Fe Depot Museum in Shawnee, Oklahoma.

Authors Ami Reeves and Carolyn Brown for their encouragement and willingness to answer my questions.

My aunt, Carolyn, for modifying the photograph.

My aunt, Joan, for her medical advice—any errors are solely my own.

My aunt, Karen, and great-aunt, Donna, for coming up with the perfect waltz.

My mother-in-law, Joyce Ann, for her knowledge of flowers.

My cousin, Travis, for helping with the steps to develop glass plates.

My husband, Andy, and our girls, Chloe and Phoebe, for their continued love, support, and excitement.

Prologue

October 1905
Wichita, Kansas

Owen Emerson paused on the front porch of Mrs. Sorenson's boardinghouse. He removed his brown derby hat, and ran shaky fingers through his hair. His hand went automatically to his suit coat pocket. The telegram was still there and it crackled as he touched it. The wire had been sent to him by the landlady's daughter, Ingrid Sorenson, informing him that his wife, Amanda, was in labor. Their first child was several weeks early. He hoped they were both well.

He and vivacious Amanda had been married less than a year and they were planning to move to Oklahoma Territory where he would work in his uncle's store. He had been there, in Shawnee, when the telegraph found him. He took the first train back. Now, here he was, standing still as a stone, afraid to go in because of what he might find.

He took a deep breath and let himself in. He smiled tentatively as Amanda's friend, Ingrid, hurried toward him.

"Owen," Ingrid said as relief washed over her face. She reached out, squeezed his arm, and ushered him in. "I'm so glad you're finally here."

"I came as soon as I could."

She took his hat and put it on the hall table. She turned back to him. She appeared tired and her blond hair wasn't as well kept as usual.

"How are they?" he asked.

"Amanda is hemorrhaging." Her troubled eyes found his. "The doctor says she will not live long."

"No . . ." He fell back a step, not sure his legs would hold him. Blood rushed in his ears. "And the baby?"

She put a hand out as if to catch him if he should tumble over. "She's small, but the doctor thinks she will be fine."

He straightened his shoulders and steeled himself against the shock of it all. "I need to see her . . . them."

Ingrid nodded. "Mother is sitting with her."

He moved by her and trudged up the worn stairs unconsciously bypassing the one that creaked. He went to the first room on the right. The door was ajar. He went into the dimly lit quarters.

Mrs. Sorenson arose from the chair next to the bed. "Mr. Emerson. I'll leave you with her," she said. She brushed past him with a rustle of skirts.

Amanda was curled up on her side in the rumpled bed. Her thin face was as pale as her white pillowcase. There were dark circles under her eyes. Her normally neat and orderly brown hair was strewn around her.

He sat next to her as quietly as he could. He took one of her cold hands that had escaped the covers. Her fingernails were blue. "Amanda?" he asked gently, not sure if he should wake her or not.

Her eyelids fluttered open at the sound of his voice. Her familiar gray eyes focused on him. "Owen?" she asked with purple lips.

"Yes. I'm here."

She rolled her head and glanced at the cradle on the other side of the bed. "Would you like to meet our daughter?"

"Of course," he said.

He went over to the cradle. The baby, so tiny and delicate, was engulfed in a white gown. She was content as she slept, unaware that her life was about to change forever.

"I named her Hope."

"Hope." He lightly stroked her downy head. Pride and affection welled up for the helpless infant. "She's beautiful."

"I thought so too." She grimaced and a hand went to her abdomen.

"Amanda . . ." He returned to her side and sat in the chair. He brushed wisps of hair from her clammy forehead. She looked so fragile. "When you're better, we'll move like we planned. You'll like Oklahoma Territory. It's the perfect place for a free spirit like you," he rambled, hoping to get her mind onto the future.

"The doctor says I'm dying . . ."

He didn't know if he was strong enough to have this conversation. "Since when have you done what people expected? You'll be up and around in no time." He tried to be cheerful.

"Not this time," she spoke softly. She closed her eyes.

"You can't, Amanda. No," he said sternly.

A single tear rolled out of the corner of her eye.

"What will I do without you?" His throat closed up. He felt choked. "How will I take care of Hope?" he whispered.

She looked at him again. "Move to Shawnee . . . your aunt will help you . . ."

"No."

"You have to do it, Owen." She weakly waved her hand like she always did when she wanted to finish a conversation.

He grabbed her hand and held it to his cheek.

"There are things I want to apologize for . . ." Her gaze held his. "I know I haven't been the best wife—"

"Stop. You've been a fine wife. I've been proud to say you're mine."

A whirlwind romance of two months had concluded with a spontaneous wedding. His young wife was flirty and fiery—everything he was not. It had been difficult getting accustomed to each other the past year. Their personalities had clashed many times, but now that their marriage was about to come to an end, Owen was terrified of the future without her.

He knelt on the floor next to her. He wiped her tear away and kissed her tenderly. "I love you, Amanda," he mumbled against her skin.

"And I love you . . . ," she breathed. A sigh escaped her lips, and she closed her eyes for a final time.

Chapter One

February 1906

Rose Dennis first noticed him as she and her best friend, Gwen Sanders, entered the train car at the Rock Island station in Oklahoma City. It would have been difficult to miss the young man trying to give a bottle to a fussy baby. His furrowed brow eased as the infant began to take in nourishment.

Rose carried her tapestry valise as she followed Gwen. Her friend picked the seat across the aisle from the father and child and plopped down. Rose put her bag in the overhead compartment and unbuttoned her long black coat. She sat and arranged her navy skirt.

"I'm so glad we'll be home soon," Gwen said. "Thanks again for going to Guthrie to visit my mother." She leaned over, their wide-brimmed hats touching, and whispered, "I knew Walter wouldn't pressure me to pick

6

a wedding date if you were with me." She pushed some stray brown hairs behind her ear. "It's not that I don't want to get married, you know. I'm just not ready to quit yet. I like being the society reporter for the newspaper."

"There's nothing wrong with waiting until you're ready," Rose affirmed. "Besides, I was happy to go on a little trip before I start my position tomorrow."

"Are you nervous?"

"A little. I wanted to work and have some independence, but I do feel anxious leaving Mother at home while she's still in such deep mourning."

"Your father's death has been really difficult for her, hasn't it?"

She nodded. "Father was quite a force in our lives. He wasn't a colonel in the Army for no reason." She gave her a sad smile.

She felt Gwen press her arm with an affectionate squeeze as the conductor called the final boarding for passengers. Two quick blasts of the whistle pierced the air as the engine erupted in a loud whoosh of steam and smoke. The train lurched and began to build momentum as it headed east toward Shawnee, Oklahoma Territory.

The noises from the train must have startled the baby because it let out a wail. The father put down the bottle and jiggled the infant in vain. A balding man in a suit peered over his shoulder and sighed audibly. The young man renewed his efforts by putting the baby to his shoulder.

Gwen leaned forward and asked in her amiable way, "Is your wife not on board to help you?"

The distraught fellow shook his head.

"We wouldn't mind helping. Would we, Rose?"

"That's not necessary. I wouldn't want to put you out." His voice was surprisingly deep.

"It's no bother at all." Gwen stood and held onto the back of the seat as she stepped over Rose's feet.

Rose followed reluctantly and sat next to Gwen opposite the young man. Her cheeks turned crimson at Gwen's boldness. It wasn't that she minded helping; it just always amazed her how confident her friend was.

Gwen had already taken over and was trying to rock the infant. When her efforts did not succeed, she handed the baby to Rose.

"Rose is wonderful with children," Gwen assured him.

The little one wore a tan cashmere cloak with a ruffled hood. Rose noticed pink embroidery peeking through on the baby's dress. "What's her name?" she found her voice to ask.

"Hope." He eyed them suspiciously.

"How lovely. How old is she?"

"Four months."

Rose nodded. She had seen plenty of babies in her life but Hope was the loveliest. Even though Hope's face was red from crying, she had a perfectly shaped nose and lips, chubby cheeks, and almond-shaped blue eyes. Rose held Hope close, patted her back rhythmically and began to hum "Oh Slumber, My Darling."

"So, you are traveling without your wife?" Gwen asked the stranger.

He cleared his throat, obviously uncomfortable. "I'm a widower."

"Oh, I'm so sorry." Gwen put her hand to her mouth. "I spoke without thinking. My fiancé is trying to cure me of that." She peeked at Rose's bundle. "It looks like she's beginning to settle, Rose."

Rose smiled at Gwen and then the stranger. When she met with his hazel eyes, she felt the color rise in her cheeks. On hearing he wasn't married, she made a concerted effort to not stare at him, but it was not easy. He was handsome in an unassuming way. His light brown hair was neatly combed back in abundant waves. He was of slight build, but had a strong chin, a prominent nose, and a chiseled mouth. She blushed again.

Gwen faced him and extended her hand. "I apologize for my thoughtlessness. I'm a reporter for the *Shawnee Globe* and too curious sometimes. My name is Gwen Sanders." She shook his hand. "This is my friend, Rose."

"Owen. Owen Emerson," he paused as his eyes held Rose's. "Nice to meet you both."

After his initial misgivings about meeting his new traveling companions, Owen could not believe his good fortune. He had taken note of the two pretty women as they stepped into the train car. Miss Sanders almost looked familiar, but he couldn't imagine where he had seen her. She was pleasing to look at, but there was something extraordinary about Rose. Her hair was a light color, like that of corn silk. Her complexion was as flawless as porcelain, except when her cheeks were stained as red as her full lips. Her face was heart shaped, and she had big blue inquisitive eyes. She appeared to be about his age and he had just turned twenty-five.

"You said you worked for the *Shawnee Globe,* Miss Sanders?" he asked. "I'm moving to Shawnee."

"Just call me Gwen. Yes, I do. You'll like Shawnee. There are at least seven or eight blocks to the downtown area. There are several churches, banks, and railroads in town too. It's a growing city."

Gwen went on to extol the virtues of the town. He tried to listen as his attention wandered from her to Rose and Hope. Gwen caught his notice, though, when she mentioned a hotel.

"Did you say the Norwood? I stayed there when I visited last October."

"October? Wasn't that when our church had that fund-raiser there?" Gwen asked Rose.

"Yes, I believe so."

"We had a costume ball at the Norwood Hotel. I was an Irish lass, and Rose was a black swan. It was a fun evening."

"I actually attended that dance. My aunt insisted that I should go." Owen's heart started to thump harder. That's why Gwen looked familiar. He had seen them at that dance. Was Rose the swan he had danced with several times that night? She had looked incredible in an elegant black dress. Her face had been covered with a feathered mask. They had agreed to wait to reveal their identities at midnight with everyone else, but the telegram had arrived about Amanda and prevented it.

He had convinced himself at the time he was just having an innocent diversion, but he realized he had been treading on dangerous ground. He had no business dancing with someone who wasn't his wife. Knowing that Amanda had been miles away about to die made him shudder with shame.

"I can't believe you were there! Wasn't it a fine evening? What was your favorite part, Rose?"

She turned red. "The music, of course."

It was her. He was positive after hearing her voice again, and that telltale blush had to mean something. The attraction must have been mutual that night. Her sweet face made him feel even guiltier. He hoped Shawnee was a big enough town that their paths wouldn't cross often. He didn't ever want her to know what a cad he had been.

Chapter Two

Rose fastened the last button on the collar of her mauve flannel shirtwaist. She brushed lint off of her dark gray wool walking skirt, stepped back, and took a final glance at herself in the full-length mirror. She appeared calm on the outside, but inside she was a wreck. It had been a big step for her to get a job, and she was so nervous.

"At least you look respectable for the first day of work," she muttered to herself. She lightly touched her upswept hair, making sure it was all in place. She glanced at the engraved silver watch pinned to her blouse and noted that it was almost time to go.

She left the sanctuary of the pink flower-papered walls and lace curtains in her room, and hurried down the narrow back staircase that landed into the kitchen. The aromas were glorious. Her mother turned from the stove where she had prepared bacon, eggs, toast, and coffee. She was wearing a navy calico wrapper, and her graying blond hair was in a loose braid down her back.

"Good morning, dear." Mrs. Dennis gave her a small smile.

"Morning, Mother." Rose kissed her cheek. "Everything smells wonderful, but I think I'm too nervous to eat it all. Will you save it for me in the icebox until lunch?"

"If that's what you'd like."

Rose sat at the small, round walnut kitchen table and placed two pieces of toasted bread on a Blue Willow breakfast plate. She slathered on pear preserves as her mother placed a steaming cup of coffee nearby. Rose poured in a generous amount of cream and spooned in sugar.

"What are you going to do today, Mother?" Rose asked before she took a sip of coffee.

She sighed. "I don't know."

Her mother had lost her drive since her father's death. She used to volunteer and spend her days actively.

"Why don't you go to the Carnegie library, or see if they need any help at the hospital?" Rose suggested.

"I might." She turned back to the stove and prepared herself a plate of food.

Rose knew her mother would not go anywhere that day, but she would keep asking. Maybe someday her mother would be herself again.

Rose quickly finished her breakfast. "I'd better go.

I don't want to be late on my first day." She placed her dishes in the sink, and gave her mother a peck on the cheek.

"Good-bye, dear. Good luck."

Rose waved, and hurried to the hall tree by the front door. She put on her black hat and ran the hat pin through. She shrugged into her long coat, buttoned it, and pulled on the red mittens that were in the pockets. She wrapped a red knitted scarf around her neck, nose, and mouth. She opened the door and stepped out into the frigid wind. She braced herself to walk in the cold the few blocks to her new job. As she did, she had the feeling she was stepping into a new life.

Owen opened the six-foot-tall wire gate to the pen. His uncle, Bob, had done a fine job building the lean-to against the back side of the redbrick store building on the west end of Main Street. The small pen had a tin roof and a southern exposure. The Rock Island train yards and tracks weren't far away but the noise didn't seem to bother his nanny goat, Nan.

"Morning, girl. How do you like your new home?" He scratched her behind the ears as she bleated and butted his leg. He dropped some hay into the bin, and she started eating. He took a stool off a high hook and put it and a clean bucket next to Nan. He squatted on the stool, patted Nan's gray-and-black back, and began to milk her like he had done for several months.

He had never farmed before, but Hope changed his

views on animal husbandry. When Hope was born she was given cow's milk, but she continued to cry and spit up every bottle. Ingrid had heard goat's milk might settle better, so he bought a goat and, thankfully, Nan's milk did seem to be better for Hope.

He wagged his head as he thought of Hope's first few months of life. It had been difficult to learn how to take care of a fussy baby and a stubborn goat. He really could not have done it without Ingrid's help. Truthfully, it was why he had stayed in Wichita so long.

He knew it was time to move on, though, when Ingrid all but proposed marriage to him. She was a friend and she had been like a sister to Amanda, but he was not going to marry out of convenience. He left before Ingrid became any more attached to Hope or him. His relationship with Amanda had been tempestuous at times. If he ever married again, he would find someone he was compatible with and head over heels in love with. Marrying only to have a mother for Hope wasn't a life he wanted.

Nan bleated and interrupted his thoughts. He finished milking so he could go back up to his apartment on the second floor of the store. Hope would probably be awake by now. It seemed she never slept for very long at a time.

He picked up the bucket of milk, returned the stool, and let himself out, latching the gate behind him. He went in through the back door and hurried up the stairs in the stockroom at the rear of the store.

He stepped onto the landing and opened the only

door upstairs at the right. He automatically glanced across the expansive room and saw Hope still sleeping peacefully.

"Good," he whispered to himself as he turned on the switch for the electric lights. He put the pail down momentarily while he removed his coat and black Brighton-style wool cap and hung them on the coat rack next to the door.

He paused to admire his new home. It was the nicest place he had lived since his parents died in the house fire when he was seventeen. His aunt Betty, his mother's sister, had done a fine job painting the walls white and cleaning the place up for him and Hope. The worn, varnished wood floors had been dutifully scrubbed and a few braided rugs were scattered here and there. The living area was to the left. She had placed a dark green secondhand sofa, a small parlor table with kerosene lamp, and a sturdy oak rocking chair under the row of windows at the front of the building. Along the wall across from the door was a carved chiffonier with a rectangular mirror at the top. Hope's large wooden cradle was at the foot of his black enameled iron bed. Betty had even bought a bright new white crocheted bedspread.

He chuckled as he realized his favorite thing about his home was the small room next to the bed that contained his very own bathtub, water closet, and a little marble lavatory. He had always shared when he lived in boardinghouses.

The door from the bathroom led into the kitchen

area. There was an ash refrigerator, a light green kitchen cabinet with a set of doors on top, a stoneware kitchen sink, a wood-burning cookstove, and a large square oak table and chairs.

Betty told him they were happy to have him there since they didn't have children of their own. His aunt and uncle had truly outdone themselves.

At that moment Hope began to stir. He had better get the milk strained and in a bottle before she awoke. Then he would get himself and Hope washed up and ready for his first day at work.

"There!" Owen muttered triumphantly as he fastened the last tiny button on Hope's delicate pink flannel dress.

She smiled up at him as she lay on the bed. An unsteady hand reached out and batted his nose.

"You think you can bully your ole dad around, huh?" He picked her up and held her over his head. She gave him a small laugh. "I guess you can, my little buttercup." He brought her down and kissed her soft cheek.

He finally felt competent with Hope. He had been all thumbs the first few months of her life. Lack of sleep and uncertainty had clouded his perspective on fatherhood for too long. He snuggled her close for a second, knowing she didn't like to be cuddled for long.

He smiled as she began to squirm and adjusted his hold on her. "Let's leave, then. It's time for me to go to work. We'll see if Aunt Betty is ready to watch you instead of the store."

He carried Hope across the room, turned off the lights, and shut the door behind him. They went down the stairs, through the stockroom, passing shelves and crates before they walked into the doorway separating the back room from the store.

The perimeter of the narrow mercantile had floor-to-ceiling shelves full of canned goods, household products, farm implements, and ready-made clothing. Long counters with glass cases on top were along either side of the building and held smaller or more expensive items like watches, jewelry, stereoscopes, and cameras. The big brass cash register and grocery scales were to the right near the large plate-glass windows and front door. Rows of bins, barrels, and short shelves took up the space in the middle of the business and were filled with everything from boots to beans. A dress goods section was at the rear of the store along with a table to cut material.

Bob looked up from stoking the wood-burning stove in the center of the room. "Mornin', Owen." He straightened his thin frame. A grin peeked out from under his thick black mustache.

"Good morning!" Betty popped up from behind the counter with a basket of mittens that she placed on top.

She bustled over, her lean figure moving easily through the displays. She smoothed a stray light brown hair back into her bun and smiled. He was still taken aback by her similarity to his mother. He never thought they looked much alike, but there was something about the way she moved her hands and laughed that was familiar. He hadn't realized how much he missed his mother until he came to Shawnee.

"Come here, little mite. Let's go upstairs." She took Hope from him. "Have a good day, you two." She began to leave, stopped, and said over her shoulder, "Don't forget Miss Dennis is coming this morning, Bob." She looked at Owen. "She'll be the extra help we need, since you'll be taking over the ordering, keeping the books, and such. And, it's always a good idea to have a woman on hand to help the ladies with their personal items." She continued on and paused again. "You can show her around, Owen. You have had a lot of experience working in a mercantile. You seemed extremely competent yesterday when we thought we were going to train you." She smiled at him and finally disappeared into the stockroom.

Bob chuckled. "She'll miss havin' the customers to talk to." He looked toward the front window. "There's Miss Dennis now. Right on time."

Bob unlocked the door and let the new clerk inside. "Come in out of the cold, Miss Dennis. Meet our nephew, Owen."

She stepped inside and began to unwrap the scarf from her face. Owen's heart skipped a beat. It was Rose, and she appeared to be as shocked as he was.

Chapter Three

Rose hoped she had regained her composure by the time she returned from hanging her hat and coat on the rack by the back door. Of all people to work with! She couldn't believe it. She never thought she would see Owen again, and now she was going to be around him almost every day. She was excited and anxious all at the same time.

Owen came toward her. She decided it was time to forget all personal thoughts and be the best employee she could be.

"I didn't know you were to be the new clerk," he said quietly.

"And I didn't realize B & B Mercantile was where you were working." She smiled.

"Bob and Betty are my aunt and uncle," he explained.

"I guess we didn't talk much on the train after Hope fell asleep."

"No." He grinned. "Although, Gwen did tell me about her job and how the two of you befriended the famous actress Ada Marsh last year."

"She's Ada Logan now." She chuckled. "Gwen is never at a loss for words."

The bell over the front door jingled as a customer entered. Mr. Burke went to assist him.

"Let me show you around and teach you how to use the register before it gets too busy," Owen informed her.

She nodded and followed him behind the counter toward the front of the store. They stopped in front of the shiny ornate cash register.

He opened a large black book that was on the counter. "This is the ledger. We keep track of each item and tally the sale. Then we enter the total in the register."

She studied the lined pages to see how everything was recorded. She then observed Owen as he demonstrated how to use the keys on the register. There were twenty-nine keys of fixed denominations from one cent to nineteen dollars and ninety-nine cents.

"I think I understand it all." She didn't sound as certain as she hoped.

"Don't be concerned. I'll be nearby all day to assist you in any way."

She returned his smile and felt her cheeks flush. How

she was going to concentrate with him around was beyond her, but she knew she had to try.

By Rose's third day, she felt comfortable with her job. Every step seemed awkward and unfamiliar at first, but she finally felt like a competent sales clerk. After a busy morning, she was refolding a bin of ladies' wool stockings when Gwen glided in. She came straight toward her.

Owen, who was assisting a tall man with the men's linen collars toward the other end of the counter, acknowledged Gwen with a wave.

"Could you help me, Miss Dennis?" Gwen joked.

"Of course, Miss Sanders. How may I be of service?" Rose asked with a grin.

"I actually could use a pair of these." She rummaged through the bin of hosiery. "So, do you like your new job, or are you ready to live off your sizable inheritance?" There was a twinkle in Gwen's eyes.

"I must say it is tempting, but I do believe I'll amuse myself here a little longer." She went along with the jesting, both of them knowing full well she had no inheritance.

Out of the corner of her eye, she noticed Owen and his customer move nearer to them.

"These seem nice and warm." Gwen placed a pair of black worsted stockings onto the counter. She leaned forward. "The main reason I came was to give you some news. The last dance we had to raise money to build the new church was such a success that the parish council decided to have another."

"Oh, how nice."

"It'll be an Independence Ball on July fourth, and it'll be a formal affair."

"That will certainly be something to look forward to."

"I can't wait." She picked up her item. "I'd better go. I need to get an article written about it for the paper."

"I'll ring you up." They walked over to the register. Rose wrote down the sale and rang up the transaction. "Thirty-five cents, please."

As Gwen was looking in her pocketbook, Owen's customer stood patiently in line behind Gwen.

Rose took Gwen's money and handed her the package.

"I'll see you at church on Sunday, if not before," Gwen said as she went out the door.

"How are you today, Miss?" The man in line tipped his hat to Rose, exposing a full head of golden hair. He had a quick smile that lit up his clear blue eyes and rather handsome face.

"I'm fine, sir. And you?"

"Fine. Extraordinary in fact."

She began to tally his items.

"I hope you won't think I'm being too bold, but I'm new in town . . . ," he began.

She glanced up at him, and he flashed a row of white teeth. She couldn't help but notice one incisor was crooked.

"My name is Richard Dobbs," he continued before

she could speak. "I happened to overhear that last customer. I'd like to inquire where the church is and find out what time services begin."

"St. Benedict's was moved recently to north Kickapoo. Mass is at ten o'clock." She finished the sale, and he took his merchandise.

"Perhaps, I'll see you there, Miss . . . ?"

"Miss Dennis." She blushed.

"I'm pleased to make your acquaintance. Have a nice day." He put a finger to the brim of his hat and left.

Rose was closing the register drawer when Mrs. Burke hurried in from the stockroom with a crying Hope. They both appeared frazzled.

"What's wrong, Betty?" Owen went to them, took Hope, and patted her back.

"I've had trouble all week getting her down for her naps, but she won't have it today." She sighed.

"I'll try." He kissed Hope's cheek. She was noticeably calmer. "I'll be back as soon as I can."

Mrs. Burke came up to her. "I don't know if I can continue on with this, Miss Dennis," she said ruefully. "God never blessed us with children of our own, and I admit I've had some angry moments about it, but maybe I don't have the temperament to be a mother."

"Oh, well . . . I'm sure it will only take a little time for such an adjustment." She tried to encourage her.

"Maybe you're right. I'll give it a little longer. Hope is a cute little mite when she's not in a temper." She seemed heartened.

The doorbell jingled. Mrs. Burke perked up when an elderly man entered. She exclaimed, "Mr. Leland, it's been ages since we've seen you! How is your rheumatism these days?" Her spark returned as she resumed familiar duties.

The following morning, Owen was reviewing the previous day's transactions. He counted the money in the drawer, re-added the ledger, and read the total on the detail strip on the register. He had hoped he had missed something from the night before, but there was no doubt about it—two dollars were missing. He would have to talk to Rose about it and he did not look forward to it.

Rose emerged from the stockroom and came up to him. Her happy demeanor disappeared when she saw the serious expression on his face.

"Is something wrong, Owen?"

"As a matter of fact, there is." He steeled himself to do his job. "I've recalculated the figures from yesterday more than once and there seems to be two dollars missing from the cash drawer."

"Oh, goodness." Her cheeks turned crimson as she realized what he could be insinuating. "You don't think I . . . stole it. Do you?"

"No, no." He reached for her hand and squeezed it, not thinking how forward the gesture was until it was too late. He let go and knew he would be blushing by now if he was prone to do. "I was only going to caution you to be more careful."

"Oh, but I am." She seemed dumfounded. "I've been concerned about handling the money from the beginning. I always count the money coming in and going out twice."

Bob was whistling as he carried a large wooden box of lanterns into the room.

"Don't worry yourself over it. Three of us use the register. Any one of us could have made a mistake."

"But two dollars is such a large amount of money to be missing." She wrung her hands.

"Did you say two dollars?" Bob piped up.

"Yes." Owen nodded.

"I'm right sorry to both of you. I took a couple of dollars out yesterday to pay a bill and I plumb forgot to write it in the ledger." He shook his head and went back to the display he was working on.

Rose sighed with relief.

"I apologize too, Rose," he offered.

"You were doing what you needed to do. I understand." She gave him a faint smile and went over to help Bob.

Owen hoped she understood. He sure didn't want her to hold anything against him.

Rose was still reflecting on the mishap with the money as the day progressed. She did not begrudge Owen at all, but she was unsure of herself again. She didn't know if she wanted to be responsible for so much money anymore.

The door opened, and she was brought out of her

reverie by her dear friends entering. Luke Logan escorted his wife, Ada, into the store. He was speaking tenderly to her as they came in; the brim of his tan ranch hat was touching the brim of her fancy black hat. They were such a striking couple.

Ada had a pale complexion and a crown of luxuriant auburn hair. She always dressed elegantly and today was no exception as she wore a russet-colored wool serge suit with a black velvet collar, black trim on the jacket, and a graduated flounced skirt. Ada undoubtedly made the outfit herself as she was an excellent seamstress.

Luke's clothing was as easy as his manner. As a farmer, he never took pains over his appearance, but since his marriage he was always clean and pressed. He was as handsome as ever with his brown hair and brown eyes. Rose still held him in high esteem after a small infatuation she had the previous year, but she couldn't be happier for the newlyweds.

"Mornin', Rose," Luke greeted her.

"How are you?" Ada took both of Rose's hands into her black gloved ones.

"I'm fine. It's so nice to see you both here."

"Wouldn't go anywhere else since our favorite clerk works here," Luke said loudly enough for Owen, who was stocking a nearby shelf with tins of tea, to hear him.

Owen stopped what he was doing and acknowledged them. "It's nice to know that, sir."

"These are my friends, Luke and Ada Logan," Rose introduced. She felt heat rising up her face as she said,

"This is Owen Emerson. Mr. and Mrs. Burke are his uncle and aunt."

The men shook hands. Rose knew Luke had seen her blush and could tell he was sizing Owen up. He must have approved because he grinned.

Owen turned to Ada. "Mrs. Logan. I saw your performance as Marguerite Gautier in *Camille* over a year ago in Wichita. Amanda . . . my late wife . . . loved the play."

"Thank you," Ada said graciously. "It seems a lifetime ago." Her emerald eyes gazed up at her husband.

Rose noticed how uncomfortable Owen was when he mentioned his wife. It was the first time he had spoken her name. Her heart sank a little when she realized how much he must miss her.

"Can you show me what kind of block planes and chisels you might have?" Luke asked Owen. "I'm goin' to try my hand at makin' some furniture."

"Certainly. Right this way."

After they had disappeared at the other corner of the store, Ada said softly, "Luke's going to build a cradle."

"How wonderful. Are you—?"

"No, not yet, but we're hoping soon," she confided. "Help me choose some material for curtains. I'm redecorating the extra bedroom, just in case."

"We have some lovely organdies and laces. Let me show you."

Rose led the way, picked out a few bolts of cloth, and laid them on the table. They heard Owen laugh at something Luke said.

Ada glanced at the men, and she whispered, "Gwen told me about Owen and his daughter. Do I sense some admiration between the two of you?"

"Oh, no. Well . . . I mean . . . he's still in mourning. And, well . . . ," she sputtered. She realized Ada saw right through her. "He *is* rather nice." She giggled.

"And, handsome." Ada nodded in agreement.

Owen happened to look up at that very moment. Rose was mortified that he caught them spying on him. He smiled back amiably.

"*And,* he has a nice smile too," Ada added. "Now, show me these yard goods before I get you in trouble with your boss."

Just before closing time, a robust woman wearing a faded calico dress, a bonnet tied around her neck, and unkempt graying hair strode in.

"May I help you?" Rose offered.

"Where's Mrs. Burke?" she asked abruptly.

"She's not available, but I can assist you."

"No, no. Mrs. Burke always takes care of me. She knows exactly what I come fer."

"I can help you, ma'am," she tried again.

"No." Her lips were set in a thin line.

Rose looked around. Owen and Mr. Burke were nowhere in sight.

"If it's a personal item, I—" She was flustered.

"I said you ain't the one who can help me," her voice began to rise.

Mr. Burke heard the commotion and came out of the stockroom.

"Good evenin', Mrs. Sylvester. I have your item right here under the counter." He pulled out a package from under the register that was wrapped with brown paper and tied with a string. "Betty thought you'd be comin' in soon and had it all ready for you. Anythin' else I can get you today?"

"Not today," she said curtly.

He finished the sale and followed her to the door, locking it behind her.

"Sorry about that, Rose. I should have warned you about her." He chuckled. "She comes in once a month to buy cigars."

"My heavens. Why was there all the secrecy about cigars?"

"She's a widow. She used to give her husband a devil of a time about smokin' 'em. When her husband passed she said she missed the smell. She took up smokin' them herself. She'd be one humiliated woman if the other church ladies ever found out."

Rose was finally able the see the humor in the situation. "I guess it takes all kinds of people to make the world go around."

"It sure does at that. Sure does."

Chapter Four

Whenen Rose arrived at work the next morning, she interrupted Owen, who was holding Hope, and Mrs. Burke. They appeared to be having a serious discussion.

"But, what will I do, Betty? I don't want some stranger to take care of Hope." Owen seemed distraught.

Rose unbuttoned her coat, took it off, and put it away. She tried to not intrude on their conversation.

"I'm truly sorry, Owen. I tried. It's just wearing me out. My shoulders ache from carrying her around all day, and I don't have the patience for it."

Mrs. Burke didn't want to watch Hope anymore? Should she offer? She really didn't enjoy working in the store as much as she thought she would.

"Owen? Mrs. Burke?" They turned to her, seeming

31

to notice her for the first time. "I wouldn't mind watching Hope."

Mrs. Burke gave her full attention. "Instead of being a clerk?"

"Yes. I . . . well . . . I have to admit I don't enjoy handling the money. And, sometimes the customers aren't as pleasant as they could be."

Mrs. Burke nodded thoughtfully. "Do you have any experience with children?"

"I've helped our neighbor, Mrs. Cornwall, with her four children quite often. She takes in wash for other people and needs help on those days. The children are all under the age of eight. I'm sure she would write a recommendation for me."

"That won't be necessary," Owen said, relief washing over his face. "You're hired."

"That sounds like a fine solution," added Mrs. Burke. "Congratulations on your new position."

"Thank you, Mrs. Burke."

"No need for formalities around here, Rose. Call me Betty. You're part of the family now." She headed toward the front of the store with a spring in her step. "I'll tell Bob about our plans."

"Let me show you around," Owen offered.

"Yes." She was all fluttery from the rapid change of events.

They climbed the stairs, and he let her into his home. The large room was divided into cozy sections.

"How nice," she said.

"It's the nicest accommodations I've had in years." He moved toward the kitchen area.

"Let me hold her so she can be familiar with me before you leave." She held out her hands and took Hope. "Good morning, Hope," she spoke in a singsong voice. "How are you today? How is little Hope today?"

The baby watched Rose's lips as she talked and began to coo.

Rose looked up and Owen smiled at her. The silence stretched and became uncomfortable.

He cleared his throat. "Normally, I'll give Hope a bottle before you arrive. So she'll need another around eleven and three." He opened the icebox and she saw several oval glass nursing bottles with white rubber nipples that were full of milk. "Cow's milk doesn't agree with her, so I milk our goat, Nan, twice a day."

He led her to the living area. "Hope still takes several naps a day. You'll have to rock her to sleep. You'll have to be careful when you lay her down, she wakes up easily. And, she usually never sleeps very long at a time."

He motioned toward the chiffonier. "Diapers, her clothes, and other baby things are in the top drawer." He pointed to a basket next to the cradle. "She has a few toys in there."

"You can still go home for lunch if you like and I'll relieve you. Or, you can bring something to eat or you could feel free to prepare anything you can find here. Just make yourself at home."

"I do have plans to have lunch with Gwen today at noon."

"Fine. I'll be up before then." He paused, looking pleased with the situation. "Any questions?"

"None that I can think of." She suddenly felt awkward being in a man's home and being told to make herself comfortable.

"Good. I'll check on the two of you today when I can. But, you know where to find me if you have any problems."

"We'll be fine," she reassured him, knowing she always felt at ease with children.

Owen leaned forward and kissed Hope. "Good-bye, buttercup. Papa will be home soon."

"Buttercup? What a sweet nickname." Rose was touched to see the affection he had for his daughter.

He seemed slightly abashed. "I used to pick buttercups for my mother when I was a boy. She used to call me that," he paused. "I had actually forgotten about that. It seems I'm remembering more about my childhood since Hope was born." He gave Hope another peck on the cheek. "I'd better go. I'll see the two of you later."

Rose watched him leave, still reveling in the change of events. She knew she would be much happier now. Her heart had gone out to the motherless child when she first met them. She had the feeling that God was orchestrating her life at that very moment.

Owen was extremely grateful that Rose was going to watch Hope. She was more than a pretty face to him since he had gotten to know her this past week. He knew she would be a wonderful caretaker for his baby. He had great admiration for Rose. More than was probably prudent.

A woman with red hair entered the store and Owen momentarily thought it was the former actress Ada Marsh Logan. He exhaled audibly when he realized it wasn't her. The last time he had seen her, thoughts of his past had come flooding back.

He had taken Amanda to see Miss Marsh in *Camille.* They had both been moved by the performance. As he tried to say good-bye at her doorstep in the wee hours, Amanda had clung to him and wept. She said she didn't want one of them to die without expressing their love for each other. She said she wanted to marry him as quickly as possible. He had been so caught up in her passionate plea that he had agreed and they were married the next morning by a justice of the peace. Now, he was afraid every time he encountered Mrs. Logan he would be reminded of his unusually impetuous behavior.

He pulled himself out of his reverie. He finished straightening some books, drew himself up, and turned to see who he could help. The fellow who had been in before and had been friendly with Rose was lingering near the pots and pans.

"May I assist you, sir?"

"I was in need of a skillet. Perhaps the young lady, Miss Dennis, could tell me the benefits of this one over that one?" he asked with a smile that was a little too friendly.

"Miss Dennis is no longer employed at the store," Owen informed him.

"What a shame." He raised his eyebrows. "A pretty young lady like that had to be good for business," he said as he strode out the door.

As Rose stepped out of B & B Mercantile, the sun was trying to peek out from behind the clouds. The temperature wasn't nearly so cold. Spring would be here soon.

She looked toward Market Street where Gwen lived at Mrs. Brown's boardinghouse. Gwen was just racing around the corner to Main Street in front of the Becker Theatre. Gwen waved, shouted a greeting, crossed the bricked street and hurried up to Rose.

"Hello, Rose. How are you today?"

"I'm just fine."

"Do you want to ride the trolley over to the English Kitchen or walk?"

"The day is nice enough, let's walk," Rose said.

Gwen put her arm through Rose's as they began their stroll. "So how was your first week at the mercantile?"

"I don't work there anymore." She tried to hide her smile.

"What?" Gwen exclaimed.

Rose giggled. "Mrs. Burke didn't want to watch Hope anymore. I offered to do it instead."

"Are you serious?" She was incredulous.

"Yes."

"What luck! I thought you seemed a little smitten with Mr. Emerson on the train. You'll get to know him in no time now."

"You act like I'm on a mad hunt for a man." She tried to appear affronted.

"Well . . . I just thought that . . . ," Gwen sputtered.

"I'm teasing." She patted Gwen's arm. "He *is* rather agreeable, and nothing melts my heart more than a man who is good to his daughter."

"I know what you mean. Does he talk about his late wife much, or what she was like?"

"No. I've only heard him mention her once. I'm afraid he feels his loss still. I don't know if he would ever be interested in me."

"At least you'll get to see him almost every day. You'll know sooner or later."

"Yes," she agreed. "Speaking of men, have you heard from Walter this week?"

Gwen nodded. "He telephoned the other day. He wants me to come for a week or so at Easter. There's some function he wants me to attend. It has something to do with the law firm he just joined. I know I should go, but I'm afraid I'm not sophisticated enough for that crowd."

"You fit in wherever you go. You'll have fun."

"I'm sure you're right." Gwen smiled. "Now, let's hurry. I'm starving!"

Sunday morning, Owen and Hope rode with Bob and Betty in their buggy to St. Benedict's church. The white clapboard church stood near the site where the new one was to be built.

He had only been to church twice since Amanda's death. He had to admit, he was a little nervous, but he wanted to be the best father he could and that included raising Hope with God in her life.

They settled into a pew near the back. He observed the congregation. He spotted Gwen with her cousin and his wife. Near the organ, he found Rose and a woman who must be her mother from the shared resemblance.

Everyone stood as the first strains of the hymn began. Owen quickly picked out Rose's flawless soprano voice. He had no idea she had such talent. He was mesmerized by her. Her singing sent shivers up his spine.

Rose thought she heard Hope fussing about halfway through the service. Her suspicions were confirmed when she glanced back and saw Owen with Hope.

When Mass was concluded, Sister Mary Louise stood before everyone could leave. The tall, robust nun with a sincere smile always wore her black-and-white habit with a graceful air.

"If I may have your attention, please?" The nun raised her hands for a moment. "I'm Sister Mary Louise. Most of you know I'm one of the teachers at the school here. I'm going to be in charge of the new adult choir. Most of us can't sing as beautifully as Miss Dennis, but we are in need of strong voices. If you would like to join, please stay for a few more minutes. Thank you."

Rose was still crimson from the public proclamation about her singing when parishioners began to file out.

"I need to stay, Mother, but I saw Mr. Emerson and Hope. I wanted you to meet them."

"There will be time for both."

As her mother spoke, the Burkes, Owen, and Hope were making their way toward them.

"Good morning," Betty greeted them warmly. "How are you today, Mrs. Dennis?"

"I'm as fine as I can be."

"I'd like you to meet my nephew, Owen, and his baby, Hope," Betty introduced.

Owen adjusted his hold on Hope and shook her mother's hand. "It's a pleasure to meet you, ma'am."

"The feeling is mutual." Her mother lightly touched Hope's rosy cheek. "So, you're the little one that stole Rose's heart," she said softly to the baby. "I see why now." She looked back to Owen. "She's lovely."

"Thank you."

Rose thought she saw a tiny spark of liveliness in her mother's eyes.

"Would you young ladies like a ride home?" Bob asked.

"I'll need to stay," Rose said as she looked at the crowd that was gathering around Sister Mary Louise. Ada and Gwen were among them. "You go on ahead, Mother. I don't know how long I'll be. I'm sure Luke and Ada will take me home."

Her mother nodded. "If it wouldn't inconvenience you, Mr. Burke."

"Course not."

They said their farewells and, as Rose went to join the other group, a warm feeling came over her. She was glad her mother was going to become acquainted with Owen and Hope.

Sister Mary Louise acknowledged Rose as she edged into the small crowd. The nun looked around and, seeing that the church was almost vacant, she said, "This must be our chorus. I thank everyone for taking time to join. We will practice Saturday afternoons for an hour at four o'clock. I know this is a new venture for our parish and I appreciate your participation."

She picked up a stack of books. "Now, if you will take a song book, we'll see what we have to work with before we go."

A few people had to share by the time the books were all passed out. A man with a ready smile near Rose offered the use of his book. Rose recognized him from somewhere. He must have been in the store at some time.

Sister Mary Louise sat at the pump organ and said, "Let's sing the hymn on page two hundred and twelve."

The small choir of seven women and four men began quietly, but by the end of the song they sounded competent.

"Well done," the nun proclaimed. "We will have a fine choir. I thank you again for your time. I'll see you here next Saturday."

Everyone began to gather their belongings, and Rose was about to join her friends when the man who shared his book stepped in front of her.

"Pardon me, miss." He held his gray felt bowler hat in front of his chest. "I don't suppose you remember me? I met you at the mercantile last week."

"Of course." She looked up at him politely.

"Richard Dobbs," he informed her with a twinkle in his eyes. "Miss Dennis, if I'm correct?"

"Yes, Rose Dennis." She was beginning to become embarrassed by his casual yet eager manner. He was lean and so tall that she had to crane her neck to see his somewhat attractive face.

"Do you require a ride home, Miss Dennis? I would be honored to give you some assistance."

She wasn't accustomed to men seeking out her company. She felt the color rising in her cheeks. "I thank you for the offer, but my friends are taking me home." She noticed Luke, Ada, and Gwen were watching and waiting for her near the door. She made a move to go.

He reached out, almost as if to stop her, but moved aside with a sweep of his hand and said, "Until next week, Miss Dennis."

She nodded and gave him a shy smile. "Yes, Mr. Dobbs." She left him behind as she joined her friends.

Luke offered her his arm as she approached. She took it as they exited the building and walked down the steps. Ada and Gwen walked ahead with their heads bent together in discussion.

"So, who was that fella?" Luke asked quietly with a brotherly-like curiosity.

"Richard Dobbs. I met him at the store. He's new in town."

"He seemed mighty interested in you."

"Yes . . . well . . . maybe. He was rather friendly." She blushed again.

"Hmmph. Well, I'll have to check out this Mr. Dobbs."

"That won't be necessary." She was touched by his concern.

"Well, we don't need any fellas hangin' around that aren't good enough for you."

She giggled. "Whatever you think."

"Anything for our darlin' Rose."

Chapter Five

Midmorning the next day, Rose was just sneaking away from the cradle where she had gently placed a sleeping Hope when Owen burst into the room. She held her finger up to her lips, glanced at the baby who was thankfully still dozing, and walked softly over to Owen.

"Your mother has called on the telephone." His eyes showed concern. "It sounded urgent."

"I wonder what's happened." She knew her mother didn't like to use the telephone. It must be important. "Excuse me."

She clattered down the stairs and took the black receiver off the top of the large oak box that was on the wall next to the back door. "Mother?" she asked loudly into the black mouthpiece.

"Rose. Something terrible has happened." She sounded distraught over the hum of the telephone connection.

"What is it?"

"Aletha Cornwall's baby has been terribly burned."

"How?" Her hand went to her throat. She was in disbelief that something horrible had again happened to that sweet family next door.

"From what I could gather, Aletha had gone across the street for just a moment to deliver Mr. Arnold's laundry. The baby was sleeping in that big rocking chair in the kitchen, little Henry was playing with a toy nearby, and the older girls were in the parlor dusting when they heard a crash and ran into the kitchen. They think Henry was trying to push the rocking chair around the room like he has before and tiny Willie rolled into the stove. Of course being two, Henry can't really explain what happened, but that's what Aletha thinks."

"Oh, no. How bad is Willie?" Her heart wrenched for the usually happy four-month-old.

"It was ghastly . . . the side of his face and body . . ."

"Is there anything I need to do?"

"I have the other children, but you might go to the hospital when you get off and be with Aletha. As you know, she doesn't have any relatives here."

"Yes. I will." Tears formed in her eyes for the woman not much older than herself. Aletha's husband, William, had died of consumption just two months before the baby was born and now this had to happen. "Good-bye, Mother," she said as she hung up the earpiece.

She turned and saw Owen standing on the stairs. Her voice wavered as she explained what happened.

"Go on and be with her," he offered.

"Are you sure?" She was torn between her neighbor and her duties.

"Of course. She needs you. We'll be fine."

She was so grateful for his compassion, but was still hesitant.

"Go, go." He brushed the air with his hands to wave her on.

"Thank you, Owen." She gave him a quick smile before gathering her belongings. She was out the back door before she had her coat buttoned.

She walked the five or so blocks as quickly as she could without breaking into a run. The new two-story clapboard building south of Woodland Park was soon in view.

As she entered, the odd antiseptic and medicinal odors assaulted her nose. A nurse came to her and Rose told her who she wanted to see. She was led into a small room with a covered window. Aletha was sitting in an uncomfortable-looking chair, head in her hands, next to a white cast-iron crib with starched white sheets. The nurse left without a word.

Aletha looked up. Her face appeared years older and her dark blond hair was unkempt. "Oh, Rose. Thank you for coming." She stood and gave her a quick hug. "I feel terrible. Just terrible." Tears streamed down her face. "I'm sick . . . and angry . . . If I'd only made sure

Willie was safe, or the girls were watching him, or if I had only taken him with me . . ."

"Accidents happen. Don't fret over it." She gently squeezed her shoulder. "How is Willie?"

"They say he'll be fine, but I don't see how." She went to the crib and gripped the top railing.

Willie was lethargic, but his eyes were moving under swollen lids and he twitched from time to time, whimpering in his sleep as he did. He was only in his diaper and the angry red burn radiated from his right cheek down to his shoulder, and to part of his chest. There were a few small blisters near his jawline and the skin was wet and peeling on his tiny shoulder.

Rose swallowed and willed her stomach to calm down.

"They gave him something to make him sleep." Aletha sounded so tired.

Rose nodded and turned her eyes to the young mother. "Is there anything I can do for you?"

"No . . . I just . . . Can you sit with me?"

"Of course." She took her hand, and Aletha held onto it as if her life depended on it.

"Thank you," she whispered.

Owen paced with Hope in front of the windows of his home. The dreary day was coming to an end and it was dusk outside. Rose, her neighbor, and baby had been on his mind all day. He wondered if Rose was still at the hospital. He hated to think of her walking home all those blocks in the dark.

"We might as well do something about it," he said under his breath to Hope.

He put the little coat and bonnet on her, grabbed a child's blanket, and went down to the telephone. He adjusted the mouthpiece, took the earpiece off and let it dangle while he turned the small crank on the side.

"Number please," the operator said as he put it to his ear.

"313."

"Yes, sir."

Momentarily, Bob answered, "Yes?"

"It's Owen. I was wondering if I could borrow your rig to take Rose home."

"You can borrow it anytime. I'll have it ready for you when you get here."

"Great."

"Betty is havin' a ladies' aid meetin' here tonight. She won't be able to watch the little one."

"That's fine. I'll take her with me."

"All right. I'll put a big basket in the buggy for her to lie in."

"Thank you. Be there soon."

"Yep."

He put his hat and coat on and went out the door, locking it behind him. They went out front to catch the trolley. He didn't have to wait long before one came by. He paid and sat down. The streetcar soon stopped on Broadway a few houses from Bob and Betty's. He walked the rest of the way.

As he came to their large white two-story house, Bob was leading his horse, Abe, and buggy out of the small carriage house.

"Sorry, the backseat's not in," Bob told him as he approached. "Took it out yesterday to haul some things from the store."

"I won't need it."

He placed Hope in a large basket on the floor. Bob had filled it with a quilt. She was beginning to fuss by the time he climbed into the green leather seats of the fringed topped surrey and took up the reins.

"I'll be back soon," he said.

"I'll be here." Bob stepped back and lightly slapped the old bay gelding's rump as it began to walk forward.

Once they were headed back toward downtown, the motion began to calm Hope and she seemed to enjoy staring at him. He reached down and tickled her under the chin. She smiled and made noises. He smiled back at her.

When they arrived at the hospital, he hopped down and hitched Abe to the rail out front before picking up Hope. It wasn't until he was going through the door that he realized he didn't remember Rose's neighbor's name. He explained his situation to the woman at the front desk. She knew right away where to take him.

He felt awkward as he knocked on the door. Here he was being impulsive again. He was just thinking he had made a mistake when the door opened. He was thankful it was Rose who answered.

He could see the surprise on her face. "I . . . wondered if you needed a ride home." He hoped he didn't sound as nervous as he was.

"That would be nice."

"Who's there, Rose?" a woman's voice asked from the interior of the room.

"It's Owen and Hope."

"Oh, the baby you've been taking care of. They can come in."

Rose introduced them. Aletha came forward and said, "Oh, she's about the same age as Willie . . ." She sighed. "Take care of her, Mr. Emerson. Never let her out of your sight." She shuddered and looked over at the crib.

He understood the urgency of her request and nodded, unable to speak.

"Owen came to take me home. Do you need me to stay?" Rose asked.

"No, you can go. Thank you for staying as long as you have."

Rose put on her coat, hat, and mittens.

"Do you need a ride too?" Owen asked.

"Oh, no. I couldn't leave," she responded. She turned weary eyes to Rose. "Tell your mother I'll telephone in the morning to check on the others and we'll decide what to do once the doctor's tell me how long Willie will have to stay here."

Rose nodded.

"Tell my children I love them, and I'll be home soon."

"I will. Try to get some rest."

"I don't know about that." She sighed again and went to sit next to Willie.

Owen, Rose, and Hope quietly let themselves out. The cool air felt good as they walked toward the carriage. Owen put Hope in her little nest, and helped Rose up. He untied the horse, and eased himself into the seat next to Rose.

She arranged her skirts and rode with her hands clasped primly around the cords of the drawstring handbag in her lap.

Owen cleared his throat. "You live on Park Street?"

"Yes."

"Do you need tomorrow off too?" he asked.

"No. I asked her and she said she would be fine."

"Good." He was at a standstill. He couldn't think of anything else to talk about. He berated himself for his rash decision to take her home. He knew that behavior had been a flaw in his past and it was something he wanted to squash.

"The weather seems to be warming some, don't you think?" Rose asked.

"Yes, it does."

The road was not extremely busy, but he tried to appear as if he were concentrating on driving. They continued on in silence. Her street was finally in view. He reined Abe to the right.

"It's that one on the left," Rose spoke up.

"I recognize it now."

The electric streetlight illuminated the modest two-story cottage as he pulled over in front of the white picket fence. Everything seemed well kept and proper.

"Thank you so much for the ride home." She gave him a shy smile. Her eyes sparkled with appreciation and what seemed like admiration.

He realized taking her home suggested he was interested in courting her. What had he done now? "Oh, well . . . yes. I heard there was a rabid dog loose." He inwardly cringed at the excuse he gave. "Better be on my way. I need to milk Nan." He sounded gruff even to his own ears.

"Good night, then." She made a motion to get out.

He hopped down to assist her so he wouldn't seem to be a complete idiot. She would not meet his gaze as she stepped down.

His hand lingered on her. "I'll see you tomorrow?" He hoped to amend his strange behavior.

"Yes. I'll be there."

He could see the confusion in her eyes. He wished he could say something, anything, to straighten out the situation. He didn't think there was a good remedy. He remained silent.

She gently took her hand from his. "Until then," she spoke as she moved away.

The scent of her perfume filled his senses as she went by. Had she always smelled of roses?

"Yes." He cleared his throat. "See you then."

He found himself staring at her as she hurried up the sidewalk and onto the white railed porch. She let herself into the lit house without looking back.

Rose Dennis was the most captivating and wholesome young woman he had ever met. How could any man be good enough for her? How could he—an unpredictable widower with an infant—have any thought of a future with Rose? He shook his head forlornly. He turned to take his daughter home.

Chapter Six

By Saturday, Rose's mother was a changed woman. Willie only spent two nights in the hospital, but Rose's mother went to Aletha's house every day to help with his care and that of the other children while Aletha made her living washing laundry. Aletha appreciated the assistance, but for her mother it was as if a spark had ignited in her. She had found a reason to pick up her spirits and felt a new zest for life.

Her mother was sitting in the tufted burgundy velour chair near the front window as Rose came down from her room. She was humming as she mended a gray shirtwaist. She looked rested and put together.

"Are you leaving for choir practice?" she asked.

"Yes," Rose answered.

"Be sure to bundle up. It's gotten cold again."

"I will." She grinned and leaned down to give her a kiss on the cheek. She straightened and glanced at the ornate walnut clock on the fireplace mantel. "I'd better go. Gwen's going to meet me at the corner." She went to the hall tree and donned her outdoor things. "I'll be back as soon as I can."

"I have bread on to rise and I'll be cooking a big pot of beef stew. Invite your friends for supper if you'd like."

"That sounds wonderful. I'll see if they have any other plans. Good-bye." She went out the door and quickly shut it behind her to keep out the wind.

Her skirts were swirling around her legs as she hurried with the wind at her back. Gwen was actually waiting for her with her arms wrapped around herself.

"Sorry I'm late," Rose apologized

"You're not late." Gwen chuckled. "I'm early. This gale made me walk more quickly than I usually do."

"It's terrible, isn't it? Let's hurry."

There wasn't much opportunity to chat as they rushed west to Kickapoo. As they turned north, a gust took their breath away. They held onto their hats and braced themselves for the long walk ahead.

A buggy drove past them, slowed, and then stopped. The man looked back at them and motioned for them to come to him. When they neared, they could hear him calling out.

"Miss Dennis! Would you and your companion like a ride to the church?" Mr. Dobbs raised his voice to be heard.

Rose and Gwen looked at each other and nodded simultaneously. They quickly helped themselves up into the one-seat buggy. Rose scooted to the middle, but tried to keep plenty of space between her and Mr. Dobbs.

"It's much too blustery for you two young ladies to be walking," he said as he slapped the reins on the back of the gray horse.

"Thank you, Mr. Dobbs," she said.

"You are quite welcome." He smiled graciously. "Surely, we are acquainted well enough to be on a first-name basis? Call me Richard."

"Yes, Richard." She introduced him to Gwen, who was full of questions as usual.

"You're new in town?" Gwen asked.

"Yes. I've been here a few weeks."

"Where are you from?"

"Oh, I've lived in Oklahoma City, Tulsa, and Guthrie. I'm a book salesman. I've been all over the territories. But, I might be ready to settle down." He glanced at Rose.

She was flattered and a little embarrassed by the insinuation.

"Guthrie, you said? My family lives in Guthrie," Gwen continued.

"I wasn't there long, but the territorial capital is a fine town."

Gwen and Richard continued their conversation while Rose listened in silence. Richard seemed extremely affable and he was easy to talk with.

"Well, ladies, we have arrived at our destination. Thank you for your lovely company."

"Thanks for the ride," Gwen said.

"You are more than welcome." He looked at Rose as he spoke. "I'd be more than happy to take you home after practice."

"That won't be necessary," Rose said.

There was a hint of surprise in Gwen's lifted eyebrow, but she confirmed, "We'll be riding with my cousin, but we appreciate the offer."

"Anytime, ladies."

"Mrs. Dennis, I do believe this is the best stew I've ever had," Luke complimented as he accepted his third bowl from her.

"Yes, it is," Ada agreed as she spread fresh butter on a still-warm piece of bread. "And your bread is heavenly. I have a terrible time making bread. It's usually a big hard lump. What is your secret?"

"There's no secret. You only need a nice warm place for the dough to rise, but not too hot, and I make my own yeast cakes. I'll give you a few if you'd like," Rose's mother said as she spooned stew into a large tan crockery bowl.

"I would love that. You would too, wouldn't you, my dear?" she asked Luke.

He nodded with his mouth full.

"I'm afraid my dear husband has fairly starved as a result of my culinary skills these last couple of months."

"Oh, now, darlin', I wouldn't say that." He winked at her. "It's good for the constitution and not to mention the teeth to chew on crusty bread and meat that's . . . er . . . well done."

They all chuckled as they sat around the kitchen table. It had been a while since they had enjoyed each other's company. It made Rose happy to see her friends together.

"If you'll pardon me, I want to take this over to Aletha and the children while it's still hot." Her mother motioned to the bowl of stew she had covered with a crisp white kitchen towel. "Make yourselves at home. I'll be back soon." She excused herself and left the younger set.

"So, Rose, what is your opinion of Mr. Richard Dobbs?" Gwen asked in her most professional demeanor.

"No one has ever claimed you were shy, have they, Gwen?" Luke asked with a grin as he smothered his bread with molasses.

"Oh, hush. We want to know, don't we, Ada?"

"He *was* particularly attentive to you this afternoon," Ada commented before she sipped her coffee.

"He seems nice," Rose said diplomatically.

"But, not as nice as Owen?" Gwen prodded.

"I wouldn't say that."

"Owen's a top-notch fella," Luke added his opinion.

"Yes," she agreed.

"So, you have a man that's mourning his wife for who knows how long and another man who is more than willing to make your acquaintance," Gwen observed. "Unless you've had any advances from Owen?"

Rose squirmed from the attention. "No. I believe he's only a courteous employer."

"I knew right away Ada was the one for me." He gave his new bride a tender smile. "I could hardly wait for her to reciprocate the feelin'. So, let a man know if you're interested. He might not be as persistent as me."

"Such sage advice, my dear." Ada's eyes twinkled as she looked over the rim of her cup.

He grinned and said amiably. "That's why I'm here, darlin'."

Even though they had only one practice, the choir sat together on Sunday. Richard positioned himself next to Rose, held the book for her, and was accommodating in every way possible. So when he offered to take her and her mother home, Rose accepted.

As Richard assisted Rose into his carriage, Owen gave her a tight smile while exiting the church. She was about to wave to him when Richard asked her a question as he helped her mother up.

"How do you think the choir is progressing, Rose?"

"Oh, I think everyone is in fine form."

He climbed up beside her. "I must say, Rose, that your voice is pure heaven. Don't you agree, Mrs. Dennis?"

"Yes. She definitely has a gift," her mother agreed.

"You should consider the operatic stage," he said as he urged the horse forward.

"I couldn't do that. I would never have the fortitude to do it."

"You should consider it," he insisted.

"Thank you, but no." She couldn't help but show her pleasure at his compliments.

He held her gaze until she glanced away.

A gust of wind hit them in the face and Rose grabbed her hat to keep it from flying away.

"You certainly look lovely in that hat, Rose," he said in a low voice as he leaned toward her ear.

"This? Really?" She felt the color rise in her cheeks. She was surprised he would notice such things. The black straw hat was beginning to fade and it was one she had freshened after her father died by putting new loops and a bow of black silk ribbon around the crown and nestling in several black roses.

"Although, I must say, you are fetching every time I've seen you," he whispered.

"You must turn left here, Mr. Dobbs," her mother interrupted.

"Certainly," he replied. "This is a pleasing community, is it not, Mrs. Dennis?"

"It is. Shawnee has grown immensely in the last few years since my husband decided to retire here."

Rose was a little relieved when Richard and her mother continued to converse. She was beginning to become uncomfortable from his lavish praise. She had never been one to accept compliments easily and his remarks were definitely making her feel awkward.

"And, where does your family reside, Mr. Dobbs?"

"I hail from Ohio. My parents and brothers and sisters still live there."

"What enticed you to come to Oklahoma Territory?"

"I read accounts of the land runs when I was young. I was fascinated by this unspoiled place. I packed up and came as soon as I was able. Being a salesman has allowed me to explore this and Indian Territory."

"How adventurous of you," her mother said.

"Well, it was fun, but I believe I've had dust under my feet long enough. I've decided to settle in Shawnee."

"You don't say?"

"Yes, ma'am. I'm in the process of buying a nice little home on Louisa Street."

"Really?" Rose asked.

He nodded proudly. "It's the white one with yellow trim. I'm thinking of repainting it. Maybe you could help me choose a color?"

"I might," she agreed tentatively.

"Turn here, Mr. Dobbs. It's the second on the left."

"You have a beautiful home, Mrs. Dennis," he said as he pulled up in front.

"Thank you."

Richard set the brake, hopped down, and hurried around to assist them to the ground.

"Would you care to join us for a roast beef dinner after church next Sunday?" her mother asked as her boot touched the street.

"I'd be delighted." His eyes sparkled as he reached for Rose's hand. "Until then?" he murmured to her.

Her mother seemed to approve of Richard. Maybe, she could relax around him now that she had another favorable opinion of him. "Yes. We will see you then."

"I will wait with great expectations."

She nodded in agreement, ducked her head, and joined her mother who was almost to the porch. Rose turned and waved. She would always remember his winning smile as he tipped his hat to her.

Chapter Seven

The second week of March was full of warmer weather and possibilities for Rose. Her steps were as light as her spirits as she arrived at the mercantile. She walked down the narrow alley between it and the furniture store. She went to the back and inserted the key Bob had given her a few days previous. She was honored that he respected her enough to entrust her with a key to his business. She let herself into the stockroom.

Owen and Betty were bent over looking at something.

Owen greeted her and motioned for Rose to go over to them. "Come see what Betty and Bob bought for Hope."

As she neared, she saw Hope lying in a baby carriage. Thin reeds of wood were arranged in curved lines. It was long enough for Hope to lie in comfortably on the sapphire-colored silk damask upholstered seat.

The back, near the handle, was cushioned and tall enough for her when she was old enough to sit up. The wheels were rubber, and a black ruffled sateen parasol topped it all off.

"Now we can take Hope around town in high style." Owen grinned.

"It's wonderful. We'll have fun won't we, Hope?" Rose asked the infant.

Hope was beginning to squirm and looked like she was not enjoying it at the moment. Owen picked her up.

"I know how tired my arms and shoulders were from carrying the mite around," Betty explained. "I thought it'd make life easier for you and Owen to take her out in the warm weather."

Rose couldn't help notice the pairing of Owen and herself. She wondered if the reference implied anything other than her employment by Owen. She assumed not.

"It will definitely be a big help," Rose said.

"Anything for our girls." Betty smiled. "I'm sure it's time to open by now. I'd better go up front." Her skirts rustled as she hurried away.

"I should go too," Owen remarked. He kissed Hope's cheek. "I'll see you soon." He handed her to Rose. "Have a nice day." His eyes held Rose's for a moment.

"You too."

The workday was about to come to an end when an excited young man entered the mercantile and rushed up to Owen.

"Sir." A young man with a cap covering his abundant curly black hair tried to catch his breath. "Sir, I just had to thank you for your help when you sold me that camera last week. The instruction book told me just what to do. I developed them and everything. Do you want to see?"

"Of course." Owen smiled at the younger fellow's enthusiasm. He took the photographs and viewed scenes of animals, local scenery, and family. "These are excellent."

"Aw, weren't nothin'. Anybody could do it." He put the pictures back into his jacket pocket. "Just wanted to tell you thanks." He grinned, tipped his cap, and was out the door as quickly as he arrived.

Owen chuckled and thought it might be a good idea to get a camera himself. Hope was a growing baby. It would be special to capture her progress.

He went to the case that held the cameras and took one of the black leather boxes out. It was a nice size, about four inches by five, and had a short, sturdy leather strap on top for a handle. The kit that came with it had everything he would need: a darkroom lamp, trays, rollers, fancy embossed cards, chemicals, and instructions.

"Why not?" he asked himself.

"Why not what?" Gwen seemed to pop out of thin air.

He smiled. "I was so absorbed that I didn't hear you come in." He held the camera up for examination. "I was deciding to buy this beauty."

"A camera? That would be fascinating." She inspected

it. "The process seems confusing to me, but I'm sure you can figure it out."

"I'll do my best," he joked.

"Well, once you're an expert could I beg you to take a photograph of me, Rose, and Ada? We've been the best of friends, but I'll be moving back to Guthrie before long, I would love to have a memento."

"I'd be honored. Maybe some Sunday after church?"

"That would be wonderful! Thank you." Her mouth turned up with pleasure.

Rose glided through the stockroom doorway carrying Hope.

"There you are, Rose," Gwen greeted. "Did you know Owen is buying a camera? And, he's going to photograph us after church. Isn't that exciting?"

"That's nice . . . but I won't be able to this Sunday."

"Really? Why?"

"Well . . ." Rose appeared to be uncomfortable. "Mother invited Richard Dobbs for lunch."

"Is that so?" Gwen raised her eyebrows.

"Yes" was her quick answer.

Owen took his baby from Rose and tried not to think about that Dobbs fellow. He must be the one who took her home after church. He didn't like the look of him, but there wasn't anything he could do about it.

"Thanks for your help today, Rose," he said abruptly. "We will see you tomorrow."

Rose seemed surprised by his dismissal, but regained

her composure and put her arm through Gwen's. She turned to her friend and said, "Let's go."

By the time they reached the sidewalk, Rose could tell Gwen was bursting to ask something.

"Do you have a probing question for me?" Rose inquired.

Gwen chuckled. "You know me too well. I was curious if Richard was your choice after all?"

She smiled. "He is for now. Mother seems to approve of him since she was the one who invited him to dinner. I thought I'd give friendly Mr. Dobbs a chance to sweep me off my feet."

The words were no sooner out of her mouth when Richard appeared in their path. She was mortified at the thought he might have heard her. She was inwardly relieved when he seemed oblivious to their conversation.

"Rose. Gwen. What a splendid surprise!" He doffed his hat. "I was returning to my temporary home at the Norwood for my evening meal at the restaurant there when I saw you lovely ladies. Would you care to join me?"

"It's so kind of you to ask, but we were going to the dressmaker's shop before they closed," Rose explained.

"Then I won't delay you any longer. Have a wonderful evening." His eyes twinkled as he gave his full attention to her. "Until Saturday?"

"Yes. I'll see you then."

He put a finger to the rim of his bowler and hurried away as if he did not want to be an imposition to them any longer.

Gwen laughed when he was out of earshot. "I don't know how he didn't hear us. His ears must have been burning," she jested.

"I know." She put her hand to her chest. "I was afraid I'd faint dead away. He seemed to come out of nowhere."

"We could have joined him and put off our errand if you wanted."

"Oh, that's fine. I'll see him in a few days. I'd rather spend some time with my dearest friend."

"I would too. I'm so glad you're helping me pick out some material for a new gown. I couldn't believe Walter said to spare no expense for it. The little soiree he wants me to attend next month must be some extravaganza."

"Ada might have better fashion sense than I do."

"I hated to drag her to town for that. Besides, I trust your judgment. You're always so thoughtfully put together."

They walked east a couple of blocks to Bell Street. They were about to cross Main Street when Rose glanced in the window of Mammoth Department Store.

"Oh, look at that hat."

"It's pretty. It looks perfect for you. Why don't we go in and you can try it on?"

Rose admired the natural straw hat with a wide brim

that was raised on the sides and slightly drooping in the front and back. It was trimmed with four large pink muslin American beauty roses and loops of black silk ribbon.

"I couldn't wear it yet, by maybe in a few months Mother wouldn't mind me putting the mourning colors behind."

"Let's go in. We have time."

"Yes, let's."

They went through the double doors into the huge multifloored department store that claimed to have thousands of pairs of shoes in stock.

"Do you want to go up to the millinery department on the second floor to see what else they might have?" Gwen asked.

"No," Rose answered as she crossed the shiny wood floors toward the window display. "This is the one."

She carefully removed it from the stand and carried it to the nearest cash register. The young male clerk rang up the sale and put it in a large pink hatbox while she rummaged in her handbag for two dollars.

Being frugal had always been in her nature. She had always made do and tried to reinvent her clothing and hats. It was exhilarating to be able to use money she had earned to buy something frivolous.

She took her purchase from him and carried the round lidded box by the string. "Now it's your turn."

She grabbed Gwen's gloved hand and led her back outside. They crossed Main Street and hurried to the dress shop that Ada had worked in for a few months before her marriage.

The bell rang over the door as they entered the narrow fully stocked store. Mrs. Parkinson looked up from her task. The thin store owner gave them a smile of recognition.

"Hello, ladies. My favorite employee didn't accompany you today?"

"Not this time," Gwen answered.

"You tell her not to be a stranger. Now, how could I assist you today?" She rustled toward them.

"I'm going to be attending a fancy function next month and I need a gown." Gwen pulled a folded, slightly crumpled sheet of paper from her pocketbook. She straightened it as best she could and said, "I saw this dress in a magazine, and thought I'd like something similar."

The drawing was of an elegant gown with a high-necked lace collar and yoke. The blouson waist had three-quarter leg-o'-mutton sleeves and ended with a medium sweep skirt. It was trimmed around the neckline, cuffs, and bottom of the skirt with ribbon.

"Yes. I have a pattern exactly like that." Mrs. Parkinson nodded in thought. "Now, to find a fabric." She led them toward the more expensive bolts of cloth. "What color were you considering?"

"I tend to go with browns to compliment my coloring, but it is a spring event. I believe I'd like a lighter color."

The three women searched through the selection of

fabrics. Rose spotted a gorgeous shiny shade of violet silk taffeta.

"What about this?" she asked as she pulled it forward.

"I like that." Gwen fingered the material.

"That would be a nice selection. We could use ecru lace and brown silk ribbon as the accent and for the broad sash with a trailing bow at the back of the waist-line," Mrs. Parkinson added.

"That would be lovely, Gwen," Rose gushed.

"It sounds wonderful. Let's do it!"

"I'll just need to take your measurements in the back room." Mrs. Parkinson automatically removed the tape measure from around her neck.

"I'll leave you some privacy, Gwen," Rose said. "I should go on home."

"Thanks for your help." Gwen gave her a quick hug. "I'll see you soon my *bonne amie.*"

"*Au revoir.*" She giggled, feeling like a fashionable Parisian as she swung her hatbox and left for the stroll home.

Chapter Eight

Owen locked the door at the front of the store. He needed to go over the receipts for the day, but he wanted to ask Rose for some assistance on another project before she went home for the evening. He would come back down and finish his work when Hope was asleep for the night.

He made his way past the merchandise in the store and stockroom and bounded up the stairs. He opened the door and found Rose leaning over the bed, putting the last pin in Hope's clean diaper drawers. She pulled down the cream-colored flannel skirt that had embroidery on the ruffle around the bottom, before picking Hope up.

Rose acknowledged him and walked toward him.

"I was hoping you could stay for a few minutes and help me with something?" Owen asked.

71

"I'd be glad to. What is it?" Curiosity filled her expression.

"I'd like to take a picture and practice developing it. Could you hold Hope for me while I photograph her?" He went to his chiffonier and took his new camera out of the second drawer.

"Where do you want her?"

"I was thinking over by the windows for the light. Maybe in the corner, with her face toward the window?"

Rose followed his instructions and held Hope in front of her with Hope's back against her chest. "Don't get me in it. I must look a fright."

Owen nodded, but he couldn't have disagreed more. The soft northern light made her hair shine and made her tranquil features glow with highlights and darkness.

He looked into his camera and adjusted his stance forward and backward. There was the slightest of smiles on Rose's lips. He began by trying to frame only Hope, but he couldn't stop himself as he pushed the lever and took a photograph of the two of them.

He looked up at Rose, slightly embarrassed that he had taken a photograph of her without her knowledge. "I'll try this one today and see how it turns out."

Rose nodded. "I'll be excited to see it."

"Oh, well, yes. Of course," he stammered.

He reached for his daughter and as he did, his fingers brushed Rose's sleeve and lingered on the back of her soft hand.

"I should leave for home," Rose spoke quietly as she slowly took her hand away from his.

He cleared his throat. "Yes. I'll see you out."

She gathered her things and wrapped a fringed, pink paisley shawl around her shoulders. He followed her down the stairs and out the back.

As she stopped outside, he said, "Thank you for your help, Rose."

"It was no trouble at all."

"Not only that, but for everything you do. I'm grateful that you're in Hope's life . . . and mine." He was not sure why he shared such sentiments with her. It was all true, but he didn't know what possessed him to tell her now.

She appeared as if she wanted to accept his compliments, but seemed unsure. She nodded and turned away.

"Good night," he said as he shut the door on her retreating figure.

Rose hurried down the alleyway so she could be home before dark. Some people didn't mind the nighttime, but she had always been wary of it.

Her mind was racing as fast as her feet were carrying her. What was Owen's intention? Was there a deeper meaning in his words or was he only being friendly? Why was this man so confusing? Just when she thought she was nothing more than an employee, he suggested something else.

What was she to do? Richard was coming to dinner in

a few days, and she had been prepared to see how a relationship with him might advance. But, now . . . How could she proceed when she had conflicting signs from Owen? Would it be foolish to wait for him? Could the attraction she felt for him from the beginning mean anything? Should she put all her hopes into Owen Emerson?

Owen glanced at Hope and noted that she was in a deep slumber. All of his work and chores were done for the evening.

He took his camera into the bathroom and set it aside. He placed the three small metal trays onto the wide edge of the lavatory sink. He had read the instructions several times the previous evening, but he perused them once more before propping the booklet behind the nickel-plated faucet. He turned on the ruby light and shut the door behind him.

He measured the chemicals, one at a time, in the graduated glass container. He added water and poured them into their sequential trays. He opened the camera, took out the glass plate and put it into the tray with the developer in it. He pulled his silver watch out of his vest pocket and noted the time. He took the plate out of the solution at the proper moment and rinsed it. He repeated the process with the different agents.

He was enthralled when the image of Rose and Hope began to emerge. As he waited for the plate to dry, he mixed more chemicals. He opened the package of sensitized paper and took out a small sheet. He placed paper under the plate and exposed the image to light. He then put the paper into the chemicals until he was finished. The photograph needed to dry and then he could paste it onto one of the fancy embossed cards. He would wake up early the next morning to complete the process.

Before he hung the photograph up to dry, he studied the portrait that he had made. It couldn't have been more perfect. It was the first time in a while that he felt a surge of pride at something he had accomplished.

"Come in," Owen's voice invited behind the closed door.

Rose noticed a faint chemical odor when she entered Owen's home the next morning. Owen must have developed his photograph like he hoped.

He was at the kitchen table with Hope sitting on his lap while he ate his breakfast of oatmeal.

"Good morning," he said cheerfully. "I'm getting a late start this morning." He motioned to another chair. "Would you care to join me?"

"I've already eaten, but I wouldn't mind a cup of coffee." She went to the cabinet and took out a white stoneware cup and saucer. She poured the dark aromatic liquid into her cup, added sugar and then cream from a small bottle that he kept separated from Hope's goat milk. She sat across the table from him.

Hope's eyes crossed as she stared at her fist. She waved it about before she found her mouth and started sucking on her knuckles.

"I saw her trying to roll over from her back to stomach the other day," he commented.

"Yes," she said excitedly. "She's been working on that, but I usually have to rescue her before she accomplishes it because she gets so frustrated."

He chuckled. "She's not known for having much patience. I must say she gets that from her mother. We were engaged for only one day when she insisted she had waited long enough. Once she made up her mind about something it was done. There was no more discussion." His eyes took on a faraway look and his smile wavered. "Some said she was headstrong and impulsive . . . She was an orphan like me and had to take care of herself early on. She always knew what she wanted. I admired that." He suddenly seemed tired as he kissed the top of Hope's head.

Rose tried to think of a way to change the subject of the conversation when she remembered his new pastime. "How did your photograph turn out?"

The light returned to his eyes. "Not bad, if I do say so myself." He pushed his bowl toward the center of the table and adjusted his hold on Hope as he stood.

He walked over to the chiffonier and she followed him. He picked up the photograph that was lying on top and handed it to her. The image was an informal portrait of her and Hope, but the effect was skillful.

"I was going to only have Hope in it, but when I saw the two of you together, I just had to take it that way," he explained. "I hope you don't mind."

"No." She looked up at him and smiled. "You made us look lovely."

"It wasn't me. It was the subjects."

She could feel herself blushing at his compliment.

"I made an extra copy if you would like it."

"Of course. I'd love to have one. Thank you, Owen."

They shared a quiet moment before he said, "I'd better go. Betty will be wondering what's happened to me." He gave Hope to her. "I'll see you two later."

"Yes. Until then."

He gave her one last glance before walking toward the coat rack by the door. He grabbed what looked to be the coat of a new gray worsted wool suit and put it on over his vest as he let himself out.

Rose examined the photograph in her hand one more time. She had always known she had pleasant features, but Owen actually made her look beautiful. Did he see her that way?

She took a deep breath to try to clear her confusion. She had always trusted her favorite verse that promised a future full of hope. She just didn't know which path she should take.

She stared at the door where he had just exited. "What does all this mean? What do I do now?"

Chapter Nine

"Mrs. Dennis, this was decidedly the finest meal I have ever indulged in," Richard commented as he discreetly wiped the corners of his mouth with a starched white napkin. "The roasted beef was fall-apart tender, the vegetables seasoned to perfection, and the spice cake was divine."

"You're much too kind, Mr. Dobbs," Rose's mother said, trying to hide her pride as she began to clear the dishes.

Her mother had outdone herself. She had put her best linen damask cloth on the table in the small dining room behind the stairs. She had laid out the best silver and the gold-rimmed English rose china. She had even put out her largest silver candelabra as a centerpiece.

"May I be of assistance, Madame?" he asked rising from his chair.

"Of course not." She motioned her head toward the doorway that led to the small vestibule by the back door. "Why don't the two of you take pleasure in this lovely day while I clean up?"

"I'll help you, Mother," Rose offered.

"No. Now off with you. Enjoy yourselves," she commanded with a smile.

"After you." Richard held out his arm and motioned toward the exit.

Rose led the way, but as she reached the door, he rushed to open it. She turned sideways so she could pass without brushing against him. They stepped down the treads of the porch together. He cordially extended his elbow, and she placed her hand in the crook of his arm as they strolled about the modestly sized yard. The daffodils and grape hyacinths were blooming along the white picket fence. Purple irises, orange tiger lilies, and an abundant amount of red, white, and pink roses would come into their glory later in the summer. On the right side of the yard at the rear was a little space for a soon-to-be planted garden. On the left side was her favorite spot of a rose arbor with a bench tucked underneath.

"The grounds are extraordinary," Richard complimented.

"My mother enjoys gardening."

They meandered toward the bench. Richard helped

her to settle on it before joining her. It was almost too cozy for her to sit so closely to a man she barely knew, but there was no changing the situation now.

"So, tell me about yourself, Rose."

"I like to sing and play the piano. There's not much else to tell except that my father passed away suddenly last September."

"You have my condolences." Sympathy exuded from his eyes.

"Thank you."

"Do you have any siblings?"

"No. It's only Mother and I now."

He nodded. "The last time I was in B & B Mercantile the young clerk said you no longer worked there."

"Yes. That's true, but I look after his baby. So, I'm still employed."

"I wouldn't think someone like you would need to labor out in the world."

"I love taking care of Hope. I wouldn't change it for anything."

"Not even if the right man came along and swept you off your feet?" He gave her a bright smile.

"Oh, well . . . I hadn't thought about that." She could feel the color rise in her cheeks.

All of the sudden, there was a huge cacophony of noise from the neighboring yard.

"What is that infernal racket?" Richard asked.

Rose giggled as she recognized the sound. She stood and went to the fence. Richard quickly followed. Aletha's children were stomping across their bare yard pretending to be a marching band. Winnie was blowing into a harmonica with all her might. Bonnie was beating an old rusty cowbell with a bent spoon and little Henry was banging on a tin pie plate with a wooden spoon. They were following Winnie around the yard oblivious of their audience.

Richard leaned toward her and said, "Why don't we retire to the parlor before we are permanently impaired by this clamor." He was so close his lips grazed her ear.

She was startled by the intimate gesture. She moved away from him and nodded before returning to the house with him close on her heels. Before she could open the door, he reached out and stopped her.

"Your demeanor has changed, Miss Dennis. Have I offended you in some way?"

"I . . . well . . ." She knew she must be the darkest shade of red by now. Her hand inadvertently went to her ear.

"I was afraid that was the reason. I do apologize, Rose. It was an absolute accident. I would never dream of making you uncomfortable."

He seemed so earnest that she gave him a small smile. He returned it with relief written on his face. He let them in, and they made their way to the parlor.

"Could I induce you to play for me before I have to take my leave?" He nodded toward the piano against the wall. "I would enjoy hearing some proper music."

The tiger oak upright piano was the most extravagant

gift she had ever received. Her parents bought it for her twelfth birthday. It was a special edition commemorating the World's Columbian Exposition. It wasn't intricately carved or fancy, but it had a wonderful sound.

"If you'd like," Rose agreed.

She went to the piano bench, lifted the seat, and took out her sheet music. She shuffled through them trying to find a nice selection. The top one was a sentimental song called "Last Night" that she had purchased after that dance in October. Another was Schumann's "Dreaming." It was too romantic. Her favorite was Franz Liszt's "Lovedream" for its glorious waves of emotion. She couldn't play that one; it was too close to her heart. She came across Liszt's "Evening Harmony." It was a lovely piece. She decided to play it. She returned the other compositions to the bench.

She propped up the sheets and sat down. Richard stood by her shoulder apparently prepared to turn the pages. She placed her fingers on the cool smooth ivory keys and began slowly building to several crescendos. She moved with the ebb and flow of the music, forgetting that she wasn't alone. Many minutes later, she finished with the final soft notes.

Silence followed. As she came out of daze, she looked around. Her mother was standing in the doorway with a damp dish towel in her hand. Her expression was wistful. "That was one of your father's favorites. It was beautiful," she said before she returned to the kitchen.

"I am entirely speechless." Richard put his hand to

his chest. "I have never been in the presence of such a virtuoso."

"I wouldn't say that. I just love to play." She wanted to dismiss the subject.

It had always been difficult for her to play for someone for the first time. Music was a profoundly personal experience. She always became absorbed by it as if she were one with the melody.

She examined his countenance and tried to decide the depth of his sincerity. She couldn't discard the impression that he was only fawning over her.

He rubbed his hands together and smiled. "I must be on my way. Tell your mother again how much I enjoyed her culinary efforts. Thank you for your performance and for your gracious company, Rose."

"You're welcome, Richard. Thank you for coming." She escorted him to the front door and opened it.

"I will await our next visit." He gave her an elegant bow before marching down the steps of the porch.

Rose found her mother in the dining room placing the final clean dish into the sideboard.

"Richard left so soon?" she asked.

"Yes."

"What a pity. I hope he enjoyed his day."

"He did. He told me to thank you again."

"He's quite the gentleman." She began to untie her apron strings. "We'll have to invite him again soon."

"Well . . . I don't know, Mother. I would like to wait awhile."

"Truly? Your father always said a person should strike while the iron is hot, but if you think it's prudent—" She appeared skeptical.

"I do. Thank you." She didn't know how to explain her reasoning at the moment. "I think I'll go see if Gwen is at home."

"Go on, dear."

"I'll be back soon," she said over her shoulder.

Rose was let into the entry way of Gwen's boarding-house by Mrs. Brown. She went up the staircase and stopped by Gwen's room at the front of the house. She rapped lightly on the door and a moment later Gwen opened it.

"I didn't expect you today," Gwen said as she ushered her in. "Your afternoon with Richard is over this early?" There was a twinkle in her eye.

She entered Gwen's simply decorated room that held a bed, a washstand, and a small chest of drawers. A writing desk was placed under the window that looked out on Market Street. A straight-backed chair and a rocking chair flanked the desk. Sheets of paper were strung across it.

"Were you busy?" Rose asked.

"Oh, no." She flapped her hand. "I was just trying to come up with ideas for that novel I want to write."

"I can come back another time."

"No. Sit. Sit," she ordered, taking a seat. "I want to know how your day was."

"It was nice."

"Nice? It wasn't fabulous, spectacular, or marvelously romantic?" Gwen grinned.

She chuckled. "No. I'm afraid not."

"What went wrong?"

"Nothing exactly." She sighed. "Richard was perfectly chivalrous. He was polite, and he was friendly."

"Everything a woman abhors," Gwen joked.

She shook her head. "I know I must sound insane. It's just that sometimes I get the feeling he's not being heartfelt with his remarks."

"Hmm." Gwen tapped her chin with her forefinger. "Does he seem dishonest?"

She thought a moment. "No."

"Well, maybe you're just not used to his demeanor."

"That could be true."

"If you want my wise advice, I'd give him a chance to win you over."

"But, there isn't any reason to rush into anything either, is there?" Rose asked.

"Of course not. There's no need to hurry and give your heart to a stranger."

"That's the way I feel. Thanks for reinforcing my thoughts."

Gwen smiled, reached over and squeezed her hand. "Anytime, Rose. What else are friends for?"

Chapter Ten

Owen tried to tie his plaid silk neck scarf for the third time. He was beginning to think he couldn't do it this morning. If he would keep his mind on the business at hand it would help.

He couldn't stop himself from imagining how well Rose and that Dobbs fellow must have gotten along the previous day. He knew he shouldn't care one whit how Rose spent her time or who she spent it with, but he couldn't curb his thoughts.

He heard a knock on his door just as he was finishing his task.

"Coming," he shouted as he hurried across the floor past Hope, who was lying on a colorful patchwork quilt playing with her feet.

He opened the door for Rose. She was wearing a pale

blue shirtwaist with lace encircling the high standing collar and a navy blue walking skirt. Her highly polished black boots clicked on the wooden floor as she entered.

"Good morning." There was a lilt in her voice and she smiled.

Her face was flushed from her morning walk. She smelled of the outdoors and her floral perfume. The air outside must have been crisp, because her sleeve was cool as she swept by him.

"How are you?" he asked.

"Just glorious. I think the weather will be divine today. I believe I'll take Hope out for a stroll this afternoon."

"That sounds nice. I wish I could join the two of you."

"Why don't you? We could go while you're on your lunch break."

He grinned. "Why not? The fresh air will do me some good."

Rose seemed pleased. Her eyes suddenly turned toward Hope. She pointed and exclaimed, "Look!"

Just as he turned toward his daughter, she arched her back, wiggled, and rolled onto her stomach.

"You did it!" Rose rushed to her and dropped to her knees. "You did it, baby." She gently rolled her back over and asked, "Can you do it again?"

Hope spent a moment or two cooing before she repeated her feat. She rested on her elbows, trying to hold her head up enough to look around.

Rose lowered herself so she was almost nose to nose

with her. "I'm so proud of you." She glanced up at him. "Aren't you proud, Papa?"

An odd sensation came over him when she used such a familiar term. He swallowed hard before turning his gaze back to his daughter. He lifted Hope, gave her a hug and kisses and said, "Yes, Papa couldn't be more proud."

Rose and Hope waited in front of the mercantile for Owen to be free. Hope was becoming frustrated in the baby carriage. Rose rolled her back and forth, hoping the motion would satisfy her. Owen emerged from the store.

"You couldn't have come at a better time," Rose said. "Hope was about to be unhappy."

"Let's move on, then. It's close to nap time; maybe she'll take one after we get going." He took over from Rose and pushed the carriage along the sidewalk.

Rose watched him covertly as they strolled eastward. There was absolutely nothing more endearing to her than to see a man delighted with fatherhood.

"I thought some popped corn sounded good. Would you like some?" Owen asked with a sly grin. "It's only five cents for two bags of buttery goodness."

She chuckled. "Who can resist that? It sounds good."

They stopped at Brown's Famous Popcorn shop. She waited while he went inside.

"I thought that was you," a male voice said from behind her. Richard went around her. He was carrying a large leather case. He glanced at the buggy. "This must be your little charge."

"Yes. This is Hope." She smiled at the baby whose eyes were beginning to droop.

"I was hoping to see you sometime. I was wondering if you could join me for lunch one day."

"Well, during the week isn't good for me." She wasn't ready to be unchaperoned around him.

"What about Sunday? I could take you and your mother to one of the fine restaurants in town."

"I'm sorry, but I have plans this Sunday."

"Saturday?" he persisted.

"I'm not sure—"

Owen inadvertently disrupted their conversation as he came up to them carrying two bags of popped corn.

"I must go now. I have an appointment. I'll see you soon, Rose," Richard declared before walking away. He gave them one last look before turning the corner.

Owen handed her a small paper sack and placed his carefully next to sleeping Hope's feet. He began to push again.

"So, how was your afternoon with that Dobbs fellow yesterday?"

"Fine," she paused, not wanting him to think she spent the entire day with Richard. "He left early."

"He did?"

She thought she saw a hint of a smile on his lips. "Yes, he did, and it didn't bother me at all," she informed him. She waited to see what his reaction would be.

He was positively cheerful as he tossed a bite into his mouth. He chewed thoughtfully and then said, "That's good. We wouldn't want the man to make a nuisance of himself."

After work one evening, Rose was in her yard pulling the first few weeds from around the rosebushes along the front porch when Richard sauntered up to the picket fence.

"Hello, there," he called out.

"Good evening, Richard." She stood and tried to brush the dirt and grass from her skirts. Her hair was coming loose from its pins, her huge straw gardening hat was askew, her apron soiled and her old boots muddied. She felt like she looked a fright.

"I'm afraid I interrupted you," he said as he came up the sidewalk.

"I was about to stop. It's almost too dark." She removed her stained gloves and placed them on the porch railing.

"I hope you don't mind my dropping by like this. We didn't get to finish our conversation the other day. Could I have the pleasure of your company on Saturday?"

"I'm afraid this Saturday isn't good. Mother and I have some errands to do before choir practice."

"I'm truly disappointed, Rose." He looked deflated.

She felt as if she was constantly coming up with excuses, so feeling a tad guilty, she asked, "Would you like to join me tonight for tea and sandwiches?" She glanced toward the house. "Mother is preparing it now. We always have enough for one more."

"Of course, I would."

They went inside. Rose left him in the parlor while she told her mother they had company. She hurried upstairs to freshen up. She put on clean shoes, took off her apron, and appraised her outfit. Her black skirt would do, but her sleeve was dirty. She put on a dove gray shirtwaist. She repinned her hair. She hurried to the bathroom and washed her hands and face, but refrained against dabbing more perfume on.

By the time she reached the kitchen, her mother was pouring hot tea from the teapot into cups with saucers. Richard was leaning familiarly against the doorjamb with his hands in his pockets. He stood to attention when she entered.

"Allow me," he said as he pulled out a chair at the kitchen table.

Rose sat down, reached for her napkin, and placed it in her lap as he held another chair for her mother. She surveyed the table as he took his seat. There were platters of yesterday's roasted chicken pulled from the bone, sliced fresh bread, home canned dill pickles, and peach preserves.

"It looks good, Mother."

"Indeed it does," Richard added. "I stopped by only to speak with Rose for a moment, but I truly appreciate your hospitality, Mrs. Dennis. A man gets tired of eating at restaurants every day."

"You're quite welcome, Mr. Dobbs." Her mother handed him the plate of bread. "What you need is a wife to cook for you."

Rose was aghast that her mother would speak so informally. She almost choked on her tea.

"Well, Mrs. Dennis, I do hope to remedy that problem as soon as I can." His eyes sparkled as he glanced at Rose.

Instead of being flattered by his innuendo, Rose was unnerved by it. This man was practically a stranger and he was hinting at marriage to her. She wanted to change the topic of conversation.

"So, Richard, what does your family think about you living in wild Oklahoma Territory?" she asked while placing meat on her bread.

"My only sibling, Walt, was a rambunctious youth so he's quite envious of my travels."

"I thought you told us before that you had brothers and sisters," Rose commented.

"No. Just Walt," he assured her as he looked her in the eye. "I must have said brother and sister-in-law."

Rose nodded. She was sure that wasn't what he had said earlier. Even though she thought it was strange, she let it drop. There was no reason to make an issue of it. At least not tonight.

Chapter Eleven

Sunday was a bright, calm, beautiful day. It was perfect for a photography expedition. After church it was agreed everyone would meet at Woodland Park. Owen would return home to get his camera and Hope's baby carriage, while the rest of the party would gather food for a picnic.

Owen gave Hope a bottle of milk before he left his house and pushed her to the park. When he arrived, Logan, Ada, Gwen, and Rose were unloading blankets, a crockery pitcher, and baskets from Logan's buggy that was parked on Broadway Street.

"Just in time," Logan hailed him. "I'm starvin'."

Gwen paused and asked them, "Do you mind if we take the photograph first? I'd hate to get any more rumpled, and I'm liable to make a mess all over myself when I eat."

"I don't mind," Owen responded.

"I guess we can wait on the vittles. I won't wilt away to nothin'," Logan agreed.

Everyone deposited their items under an oak tree and Rose moved sleeping Hope into the shade, while Owen scouted a good location. His first thought was in front of the Carnegie Library, but they would have to move all of their belongings. He finally decided in front of a stand of trees nearby would be ideal. The dark background would show off the ladies' light-colored dresses.

As they neared, he pointed to the spot. "That's good there. Logan, stand in the middle with the ladies on either side," he instructed.

"If you insist." He grinned.

They shuffled around finally taking their positions. Rose was wearing a robin's egg blue dress with a high collar and accented with white lace on the collar and cuffs. He hadn't ever seen her in it before. She stood on the left, holding a black parasol to shield herself and Ada from the sun. Ada was total elegance in a filmy white lace concoction. It appeared Logan was wearing his finest suit, tie, and fedora. Gwen finished out the scene with a hand on her hip wearing a white shirtwaist, a tan plaid skirt, and a wide black belt.

He tried to ignore how lovely Rose looked and put his mind back on the business at hand. He bent his head and peered through the viewfinder of his camera.

"Move together a bit more," he directed. "Fine. One,

two, three—now." He pushed the lever and it was done. "That's it." He glanced up, and they began to move again.

"Thank you so much, Owen," Gwen said as she came up to him.

"You're welcome. If it turns out, I'll make enough copies for everyone."

"That would be wonderful." She put her arm amiably through his. "Now, let's go eat," she spoke softly enough so only he could hear. "I'm starving too."

The entire entourage strolled back to their area. Logan and Owen unfolded two old quilts and arranged them on the bright green grass of spring. The women unloaded the baskets and before long an appealing meal of cold ham, bread, Boston baked beans, potato salad, and peach cobbler was laid out.

"So this is what all the commotion in Rose's kitchen was about last night? It looks mighty tasty." Logan admired the fare.

"Yes, it does," Owen agreed. He didn't know when he'd had a meal cooked by someone else. He was looking forward to it as he and Logan sat down.

The young ladies joined them in a circular pattern. Rose sat beside him and arranged her skirts in a pretty fashion. He had never been as aware of her presence as he was today.

Food and drinks were passed around. He greatly enjoyed the meal and the company.

"Do you remember the first meal we cooked together, Gwen?" Logan asked before taking a bite of his sandwich.

She gave a surprised chuckle and said, "Let's see. I was about eight and you were fifteen," she began.

"We decided we had a hankerin' for crawdads, so we met up at the creek between our properties in Kansas. I brought a supply of matches—"

"And I snuck out my mother's best cast-iron skillet in a raggedy old gunny sack. I had to drag it all the way down there," Gwen added.

"We had all matter of fun tippin' rocks and catchin' those crayfish. It didn't take long before we had a fine mess of them. I got a fire goin', and as we put them in the pan, we realized we didn't have any lard to fry them, so we dipped up some of that muddy creek water and boiled them. They were darn good as I recall."

"I agree, but my mother was madder than a wet hen when she found her rusted pan the next week while she was cutting across to your house."

Logan laughed. "My Pa wasn't so thrilled to see the ashes of a fire so close to his hay field either."

A broad smile crossed Ada's face. "I don't know how you two survived to adulthood after all your shenanigans."

"It was a lot of hard work and prayer on our parents' part to be sure," Gwen commented with a wry smile.

Their laughter must have disturbed Hope, because she

began to stir. Owen started to get up, but Rose lightly touched his sleeve and went to get Hope.

"That reminds me. I guess we're goin' to get one of those whoop-and-holler contraptions out at our place," Logan said.

"How in the world did a waking baby make you think of a telephone?" Gwen asked with eyebrows raised.

"I told him I'd like to have one if we are blessed with children. We could telephone a doctor instead of Luke having to ride for one," Ada explained.

"Next thing you know, she'll talk me into gettin' electricity at our house." He tried to grumble, but he gave his wife an affectionate smile.

"Poor Luke," Gwen said. "He has to join us in the twentieth century whether he wants to or not."

Everyone set to work cleaning up and afterward there was a unanimous decision to stroll around the park. Rose was going to push Hope in the baby carriage, but Owen gently motioned her aside noting the rough terrain. The group walked five abreast when possible, and they had a merry time as they went through the trees.

Rose was so pleased to see Owen relaxing and having fun with her friends. He was like her in so many ways. He didn't need to be the center of attention, but he seemed to appreciate a good laugh and he added to the conversations when he had the opportunity.

After a long while, they came across a bench and it

was agreed to rest for a time. Rose took a seat at the end and Ada and Gwen followed suit. Luke lounged against a tree with his hands in his pockets. Owen picked up Hope.

"Do you think she'll let me hold her?" Ada asked.

"I don't see why not," Owen said as he went to her.

Ada took the squirming baby and adjusted her hold on her until Hope was content. "She's a beautiful baby," Ada told him.

"Thank you." A wide smile broke across his face. "I know already that I'll have to find a big stick to beat off all the suitors she'll have." He sat with his back to a tree, forearms resting on his knees.

Ada chuckled. "No doubt."

"Speaking of beating off a crowd—" Gwen began. "I'm sure you've all read in the newspaper of Sarah Bernhardt's farewell tour of America? It sounds like there are terrific crowds wherever she goes."

"Is she that French actress?" Luke asked.

"Yes," Ada replied. "She is world renowned."

"Well, I just found out that Sarah Bernhardt is coming to perform in Shawnee the first week in April," she said excitedly.

"Are you serious?" Ada asked.

"Yes. There are only two towns in Oklahoma Territory that she's coming to and Shawnee is one!"

"That is *amazing*. Her talent is supposed to be unsurpassed." Ada seemed impressed.

"She can't be any better than you, darlin'," Luke said with pride.

"I'm afraid you're biased, my dear. Besides, you've never even seen me perform."

"Maybe so, but she'd have to be mighty good to impress me."

"Does that mean we'll go?" Gwen asked.

"Don't see why not. We should see what all the fuss is about," Luke assented.

"Do you think we should support someone with such a sullied reputation?" Rose asked. "I read that an archbishop in Canada forbid his congregation to go to her performance."

"It is apparently true that Madame Sarah has liaisons with her leading men," Ada agreed.

"I understand your misgivings, Rose. But, what an opportunity this is! She's coming *here* of all places. We'll never have a chance to see someone so famous." She glanced at Ada. "No offense, Ada."

"None taken." She smiled and then turned to Rose. "I have to admit, I'm extremely curious to see her. And, it's not like we're inviting her over for tea."

"What do you think, Rose?" Gwen leaned forward to watch her expression.

"Well . . ."

"It won't be any fun without you," Gwen encouraged.

Rose nodded slowly. "I'll go."

"That's settled. We'll all go." Gwen turned to Owen. "You'll come with us, won't you?"

He gazed at Rose momentarily before replying, "I would enjoy that."

Rose could feel herself blushing. Did he mean he would enjoy it because of her or only because it would be a night out? She wished she could read his mind.

"What fun we'll have." Gwen rubbed her hands together. "I'll have to see if Walter can come down for it."

"Walter is your fiancé?" Owen asked.

"Yes. He lives in Guthrie," Gwen answered. "You moved here from Wichita. Is that where you grew up?"

"No. I'm from Winfield, Kansas. My father was a bank teller. We lived down the street in a little house with a fantastic flower garden. My mother was quite proud of it, although my brothers and I didn't appreciate it as much as we could have. I was more interested in the insects I could find there." He wagged his head. "I frightened her more than once hiding bugs in all kinds of containers around the house."

"What kinds of critters did you catch?" Luke grinned.

"Everything. I think I startled her the most with a tin coffee canister full of buzzing bees. I don't know who was madder, her or the bees." He chuckled.

"How in the world did you catch a bunch of bees?" Gwen asked in awe.

"I would nab one, put the lid on, shake it until it was unconscious, then get the next one."

Everyone laughed. "That's downright ingenious if you ask me," Luke commented.

"Insects weren't the only things I'd find in the garden. I'll never forget the time I nearly gave our neighbor lady a stroke when I went to her door with a little green snake crawling though my curls."

"No. You didn't." Rose put her hand to her heart, but she smiled at the description of his childhood antics.

"I'm afraid so." His eyes sparkled. "I don't think she ever did forgive me."

"What made you leave such an idyllic life?" Gwen wondered.

His expression suddenly grew somber. "One evening, the winter I was seventeen, I had spent the night at a friend's house. My family was killed in a house fire that night. They thought the old brick chimney sent sparks into the attic . . . I couldn't stay in that town after that. So, I went to Wichita. I made it on my own for several years, until I married Amanda. Now, I have a treasure I never thought possible."

Owen's eyes were misty as he looked at his daughter. He'd been through so much. Rose wondered if she should question his seeming lack of interest in her. Could she blame him if he didn't want to love again? She knew she couldn't.

Chapter Twelve

The next couple of weeks became routine for Rose and passed quickly. She devoted her days to Hope and spent quiet moments conversing with Owen. She received her copy of the group photograph and was awed by what a good job Owen had done.

She allowed Richard to drive her and Gwen to and from chorus practice on Saturdays, but refrained from inviting him to dinner or accepting his requests to dine out. She couldn't put a finger on her reasons why she didn't want to spend too much time with him, but, oddly enough, she was also beginning to feel guilty for constantly coming up with excuses.

There was quite a stir in town the morning Sarah Bernhardt arrived from Oklahoma City. Gwen had gone to see the commotion and had returned to tell Rose all about it. Madame Bernhardt had a special train that consisted of her own private car for her company and two baggage cars loaded with stage scenery and trunks of costumes. The train was transferred to the Rock Island tracks and her "palace" cars were sent to the west yards for privacy.

As Rose was getting ready for the elegant evening out, she smiled as she remembered how thrilled Gwen was to be going to see the "divine" Sarah. Rose had to admit that she was excited, but it wasn't from the thought of seeing some actress, it was because she was going to be spending more time with Owen. She kept telling herself there was no use getting her hopes up as far as he was concerned, but she couldn't help it. She enjoyed being around him even if he never regarded her with anything more than friendship.

She appraised herself in the full-length mirror in her room one last time. She had donned a mauve silk gown from the previous season. It had a cutout neckline and short sleeves surrounded with fine white lace. To freshen it, she had sewn faux pearls around the yoke and hem. A wide pink ribbon sash was tied at her waist.

She put on a short choker of pearls. She checked the pearl-encrusted pompadour comb that curved around the knot of hair on the top of her head to see if it was secure. She pulled on her elbow-length white satin gloves and knew she was ready.

She picked up her white Shetland wool shawl with pink fringe off the bed and threw it over her arm. She went down the stairs and found her mother at the kitchen table reading the newspaper.

She laid the paper aside. "Don't you look lovely, my dear." A proud smile crossed her lips. "Wouldn't Richard be impressed to see you?"

"Maybe."

"I still don't understand why you aren't attending the theater with him." Her mother leaned back in her chair and crossed her arms.

"I told you that Owen is going."

"Why should that matter? He is your employer."

"I know." Rose tried to decide quickly how much she wanted to tell her. "I thought it would be awkward, that's all."

Her mother didn't appear to be satisfied with that answer, but let it drop.

"I'm going to wait outside." Rose gave her a peck on the cheek. "I'll be back as soon as I can."

"Have fun, dear."

Rose hurried out the door before her mother could question her any more. She couldn't explain anything to her when she wasn't even sure herself how she felt about Owen or Richard.

Just as she came to the end of the walkway, Luke's carriage was approaching. He reined his horse over. He hopped down to help her up and commented about her appearance as he did.

"Yes. You're just beautiful," Ada added from the front seat.

"So are you," Rose said as she noted Ada's burgundy dress with jet beads.

"Thank you, it's one of Luke's favorites," she commented as he joined her.

He snapped the leather straps across the back of the horse and they headed toward Gwen's residence.

When they arrived, Gwen rushed out of the boardinghouse, slamming the door behind her. She was wearing the newly completed gown that Mrs. Parkinson had made for her. She was the picture of elegance except for the fact that her skirts were flying in her wake as she dashed down the sidewalk.

There was a chorus of compliments for Gwen. She accepted it with the flap of a hand.

"It's the nicest thing I own. I was going to save it for Guthrie, but it'll still be new for Walter."

"So, he couldn't come after all?" Rose asked.

"No. He has to work tomorrow."

Luke, who had been peering ahead, said, "We should probably walk the rest of the way, ladies. I don't think we could get much closer."

"Yes, let's. The weather is nice and it's only a block and a half," Ada agreed.

Rose and Ada dismounted as Luke tied the reins to a hitching post and they made their way to Main Street. Buggies lined the streets toward Becker Theatre and traffic was congested.

When they turned the corner from Market Street, they found Owen in front of the theater waiting patiently for them. He was wearing a black worsted cutaway frock coat and trousers with a starched white shirt and collar with a white bowtie. He seemed awestruck by their appearance.

It took him a moment before he tipped is black derby and said, "You ladies are a wonder to behold."

Rose felt like his eyes rested on her longer than the others, but she couldn't be sure. She wanted to tell him how handsome he looked, but the opportunity and her nerve passed by the time they entered. They each paid the hefty price of five dollars for a ticket.

"That much money would feed a family for a week," Luke grumbled. "This better be one spectacular performance."

"Don't worry, dear cousin. It'll be worth it," Gwen comforted him.

They made their way through the crowd that hummed with recognition as Ada passed through. Sarah Bernhardt wasn't the only popular actress in town.

The simple facade of the redbrick building relayed no inkling of the splendid interior of the newly built Becker Theatre. They entered onto the sloped main floor, which was only fourteen rows from the stage, making every seat a good one. There were enclosed boxes on either side of the stage with brass railings. The two-tiered balcony was decorated with ornate gilded plaster swags.

"There must be over a thousand people here." Luke let out a low whistle.

They took their seats in front of one of three large columns supporting the balcony. Gwen scooted in first, followed by Luke and Ada. Rose settled next to her and Owen took his place beside Rose.

Rose was all too aware of Owen's presence next to her. Their elbows touched briefly on the armrest before she shied away and put her arms closer to her body. She flipped through the program to try to clear her senses of his Bay Rum aftershave. She read the English synopsis of Alexander Dumas Junior's French play *Camille*. The story was about a kept woman who was separated from her true love only to be reunited on her deathbed.

"Just ask if there is any need for interpretation of a scene," Ada told them as the lights dimmed and the orchestra began to play.

The curtain raised and the audience applauded at the first sight of the famous actress. She wore a white flowing gown and her fair wavy hair was arranged artfully. She was petite and graceful and had the patrons mesmerized as soon as she uttered her first words.

"It's unfathomable that she's more than sixty years of age, isn't it?" Ada whispered in Rose's ear.

She shook her head. "It doesn't seem possible. She seems *much* younger."

Through the actor's gestures and Ada's side comments, Rose was able to follow the story easily. Madame Bernhardt's acting was subtle yet powerful as the repentant sinner. Even though she had some reservations about

the storyline, Rose had to admit she enjoyed the performance, which was enhanced by the orchestra playing
Verdi at the most touching moments.

Before she knew it, the play was over with most of
the audience in tears. Applause thundered through the
theater. Wreaths and flowers were tossed onstage as
Madame Bernhardt made her many curtain calls. She
stood with hands on cheeks, seeming to revel in the admiration before stretching her arms out and dropping
down into a low curtsy.

After the final bows, the crowd began filing out, but
Rose and her friends remained as they were.

"I'd love to try to get an interview." Gwen glowed as
she unabashedly wiped her tears. "Do you think if you
went with me, Ada, I'd have a chance?"

"I doubt she would know who I am, but you can see
if my name will help."

"Wonderful!" Gwen dug her small notebook and pencil out of her handbag. "I'll be back soon." She stood
and tried to make her way against the stream of people
that were leaving.

"So, what did everyone think?" Ada asked.

"I'll admit that little French gal was pretty good,"
Luke said.

Owen, who had been quieter than usual the entire evening, cleared his throat. "Well, she was nice, but I enjoyed
your rendition better. My wife had been entirely taken in
by your version."

"I liked it, but all the popular romances seem to have

a tragic finale. I must be unsophisticated. I like happy endings," Rose said.

Ada smiled. "We did our share of dramas in my company, but I have to admit, I like happy endings too." She glanced at Luke and squeezed his hand. She leaned toward him and began to speak to her husband privately.

Rose turned toward Owen. "Did you and your wife go to the theater often?"

His hands trembled as he fumbled with the hat in his lap. He didn't look at her. "Yes . . . she liked immersing herself in the characters' lives," he said with a shaky voice.

Just then, Gwen returned looking crestfallen. "They said Madame Sarah left already. They said her reccurring injury required her to go rest." She shrugged. "I guess we might as well all go home."

Chapter Thirteen

Owen said farewell to his companions and all but ran across the street and down the alley to his home. He unlocked the back door of the mercantile and raced up the stairs, yanking off his bowtie and undoing the high-necked collar that was choking him.

He entered quietly, and ushered Bob and Betty out with hushed tones. He couldn't stand to be in anyone else's company a second longer. He put his hat and coat on the rack and noted that Hope was sleeping in her cradle.

He pressed his forehead against the door. The death scene in the play had been more than he could bear. Tears that he had never had time to shed for Amanda came rushing out.

"Why?" he asked angrily. "Why did you have to die?

Why did you have to leave me all alone with a baby to take care of?"

Grief engulfed him. His chest hurt so that he felt it might burst. He turned, leaned against the hard wood, and slid down to the floor. With his elbows on his knees, he gripped his forehead and tried to squeeze out the memories that were flooding in.

Amanda had been full of vitality, amusing, occasionally brash, and passionate in every way. He was just getting to learn all the facets of her when she passed away. How could losing someone you'd known about a year be so painful?

During their marriage, he had always felt he was swimming in her wake, as if he was always trying to catch up with her. He never felt he appreciated her enough or loved her enough. He always thought he hadn't given her all his devotion. He never quite opened his heart to her fully.

So, when he hadn't cried at her funeral he assumed he hadn't loved her well. He realized, now, that he had stuffed all his emotions aside so he could take care of their baby. And, even though she may not have had every corner of his heart, the pain he felt over her death was real.

"What do I do now, Amanda?" He took a shuddery breath.

His head fell back against the door as he remembered the evening. Rose had been breathtaking. She was grace and light and gentleness. Everything that had been missing in his life since his mother died.

He could just imagine Amanda laughing and teasing him. She would have said he was a coward. He wanted to love someone utterly and completely. Could he be brave enough to try? Was Rose the one? He didn't know, and he was too weary to figure it out.

He hauled himself to his feet and trudged over to the chest of drawers. As he took out his night clothes, he remembered the photograph of Amanda he had hidden in the back of a drawer. He unearthed it and stared at her vibrant face in the dim light. It had been taken before they had met. Even though she only had the faintest of smiles, the photographer had captured the mischievous gleam in her eye. He was startled when he realized there was only a small ache of longing for her. Maybe he was ready to start again. He knew Amanda would encourage him to do so.

He carefully leaned the photograph against the mirror. Hope should know all about her mother. He felt that he could do it now.

Rose noticed that Owen looked bleary-eyed when he let her in the next morning. He was still able to greet her with a warm smile, though.

"Come in. I'm not quite ready for work, yet. It was a late night, wasn't it?" He ran his fingers through his disheveled wavy hair that needed a touch of pomade to get it under control.

"Yes. It was."

He rubbed the light-colored stubble on his chin. "I'd better go finish up."

She was relieved when he turned away. His collar was open and his gray undershirt was peeking out. She had been having difficulty refraining herself from staring at the curves of his neck and wondering how soft it would feel.

"I think Hope might need a new diaper. If you don't mind . . . ," he said over his shoulder as he put his arms through each dangling suspender and shrugged them on.

"I'll take care of her."

She walked to the chiffonier and spoke to Hope, who was playing with her feet on a blanket, as she passed. When she was pulling out the top drawer, she noticed the likeness of a young woman against the mirror. She picked it up. The figure staring back had dark hair, an oval face, and full lips that looked ready to smile, and engaging eyes. She was beautiful. It must have been Owen's wife. She replaced the image, wondering what its sudden appearance signified.

She went to Hope and changed her sodden diaper. Owen emerged looking all put together. His hair was under control, his collar was buttoned, his bowtie was on, his face smooth and he smelled of shaving soap.

She picked Hope up and stood. She knew it was forward, but she had to see what his reaction would be. She nodded toward the dresser and asked, "I saw that picture. Was that your wife?"

"Yes." He swallowed before continuing. "That was Amanda. I realized that Hope should know who her mother was."

Silence stretched before Rose could summon the courage to ask the question that had been gnawing at her. "It won't make you miserable to see it every day?"

He let out a long, low sigh before looking her in the eyes. "I don't think so."

Her heart fluttered. "I hope not."

Easter Sunday was a fine day. The sun shone with a slight breeze to make the day comfortable. The church was handsomely decorated with palms, ferns, cut flowers, and potted plants. The ladies of the church had truly outdone themselves. The choir sounded particularly melodious that morning, and Rose was proud to be a part of it.

As the congregation departed the crowded church, Rose waved to Owen and Hope, but was unable to get to them. Her mother made her way toward Rose, Ada, Luke, and Richard.

"Good morning, Mrs. Dennis," Ada greeted.

"I hope you are all well this morning," her mother said to them. "I'm counting on all of you joining us for roasted leg of lamb for lunch."

"Don't know how we could refuse such an invitation. Don't you agree, Ada?" Luke rubbed his hands together with a hopeful look on his face.

"We'd love to," Ada consented.

"I greatly appreciate the invitation, Mrs. Dennis. And I heartily accept," Richard said with his hand to his chest.

"Where is Gwen? She can come too," her mother said.

"She went to visit her family and Walter a few days ago," Rose informed her.

"Oh, that's right. I'd forgotten." She moved toward the door. "Come along, everyone."

They followed her out. Richard drove Rose and her mother while Luke and Ada arrived in their own buggy.

Her mother insisted that Rose visit with their company while she finished preparing the meal. Rose took her friends to the back porch. She and Ada sat in the white wicker chairs while Luke lounged against the railing. Richard appeared to consider his options and finally sat on the top step, turning sideways to face the women while leaning back on the post.

"So, how long have you been in Shawnee, Dobbs?" Luke asked.

"A few months," Richard answered.

"Where were you before you came here?" Ada entered the discourse.

"Here and there," he said politely, but didn't seem to care to expand on it.

"He said he is buying the house with yellow trim on Louisa Street," Rose said, hoping to make the conversation flow better.

"Really? Isn't that old man Benson's house?" Luke inquired.

"Yes . . . But, he changed his mind," Richard said. "So, I'm still looking for a property."

"Hmm." Luke crossed his arms and eyed him warily.

"So, how does the famous Ada Marsh enjoy living in this little burg?" Richard turned the focus onto Ada.

"I love it. I've found almost everyone extremely hospitable."

"Yes. I'd agree. Most people are quite courteous."

Rose thought she saw a flicker of annoyance as Richard glanced at Luke. She doubted what she saw, though, when Richard's countenance remained pleasant.

Richard turned his attention to her. "I read in the newspaper that the carnival is coming to town next week. You'll accompany me, won't you?"

"Yes. I suppose I could go one evening after work."

"How does Thursday sound?"

"That would be fine." She gave him a tentative smile, and he reciprocated, looking quite pleased.

"Will Gwen be back by then to chaperone?" Luke asked suspiciously.

"She won't return until Friday." Rose was flattered and slightly amused by Luke's concern.

Richard stood slowly. "I assure you, Logan, the lady has nothing to fear. I shall be chivalrous as always."

"I still don't think it's fittin' for a young lady to be unescorted with a man she barely knows," Luke said boldly.

"If you intend to offend me—" He stepped forward, glaring at Luke.

Rose jumped to her feet. "I'm sure Luke didn't mean to slight you, Richard. He's a dear friend and like a brother to me." She turned to Luke. "Now, Luke, we'll be out in public, and I'm sure Richard will be nothing less than a gentleman."

How could a simple chat have escalated to this? She was appalled that an argument was about to break out on her porch. She watched the two men slowly back down.

Finally, Luke unfolded his arms and stretched out a hand. "No harm meant."

Richard nodded and shook his hand.

"Now, let's not spoil this lovely day. Let's take a stroll before dinner," Rose requested.

"Yes, let's." Ada gave Luke a scolding glance as she arose and took her husband's arm.

"As you wish." Richard bowed and let Rose proceed in front of him down the steps.

"Rose?" Luke asked.

She turned and looked back at him. He broke away from Ada and came to her side, leaving Ada and Richard waiting on the porch.

He leaned forward with a sheepish expression and whispered, "Sorry. I didn't mean to embarrass you. I'll behave myself from now on."

"You'd better," she spoke softly. A smile crossed her lips. "But, I do appreciate you looking out for me." She raised her head and said to all, "Now, let's go have a little diversion."

Chapter Fourteen

Wednesday, the eighteenth day of April, was a day that would live in the minds of Rose and her friends for the rest of their lives. Owen told her at lunchtime that there were rumors of a large earthquake in San Francisco. The gravity of the situation wasn't truly known until the evening edition of the *Shawnee Globe* came out. More than a thousand buildings had been destroyed, fires were overtaking the city, all the telephone and telegraph lines were down, water and sewage pipes were broken and spewing into the streets. It was speculated that over two hundred fifty thousand were homeless and over two thousand dead.

Rose's heart went out to the city and its inhabitants as she stood next to Owen and read the newspaper that was spread across the kitchen table.

"How absolutely terrible," Rose murmured.

"It's difficult to imagine such a tragedy," Owen agreed.

"Where will all those people go? How will they find food to eat?" She shifted Hope from one hip to the other.

"I don't know." He shook his head.

"We have to do something."

"What could we do from here?"

"We . . . we could have a food drive."

"That's a wonderful idea!" he said excitedly. "I'll bet Bob and Betty will get the donations started."

"I'll telephone and visit all the church ladies."

"I think Bob knows an engineer from the Rock Island Railroad. Surely they can find a way to get it there."

"I'll start calling everyone now." She handed Hope to him.

"And I'll go talk to Bob and Betty," he stated as they headed toward the door together.

The next day was a flurry of activity. Word spread quickly and people from all over town were bringing donations to the stockroom of Bob and Betty's store. Owen took time from his regular duties to help Rose crate all the items. Canned goods, sacks of flour, beans, oatmeal, rice; and tins of tea and coffee poured in. Clothes of all sizes were also brought in.

Rose was so proud of the generosity of the community. She bought what she could, but still wished she could do more. She was touched beyond measure when her mother arrived with a huge armload of her father's clothes. There had been a hint of tears in her eyes when she handed them over, but she assured Rose she was ready to give them to someone who needed them.

It was a busy day, but one that passed quickly. Rose stayed well after closing time as items were still being dropped off.

She was folding garments when another knock came. She pushed back some stray hairs that had come from their pins and went to answer the door.

"This'll have to be the last one for the day," Owen said as he picked Hope up off a quilt on the floor. "Hope and I are hungry."

"Me too." She gave him a tired smile over her shoulder. She was taken by surprise when she found Richard standing there.

"Richard." She tried to not seem too startled.

"Your mother told me you would probably still be here. Are you ready to go?"

"Ready?" She tried to figure out what he was talking about.

"Don't tell me you forgot our engagement?" He placed his hand over his heart.

"Oh, I . . . I've been so busy it did slip my mind." She took off the grungy white shop apron and hoped her white shirtwaist and navy skirt weren't too rumpled. She hung the apron on a hook by the telephone. "I apologize."

"You'll still attend with me, won't you? I'll be going out of town tomorrow for a few days. You surely won't deprive me of your company before I go?" His eyes implored hers.

"Well, no . . . of course not." She retrieved her hat. She couldn't look directly at Owen as she said, "I'll see you in the morning." She ducked out as he quietly said good-bye.

Richard led her to his buggy, and they rode the few blocks to a lot near the old Choctaw passenger depot. The electric lights, the appetizing aromas of food, and the shouts of glee were evident before they rounded the corner of Union Street. They entered the bustle of the carnival and stood momentarily wondering which way to go.

"So, would you like to be awed by the great Rosey the Marvelous Unicyclist or Illumino the Human Electric Light who walks on a live electric wire?" Richard asked as he rubbed his hands together.

"Actually, I don't care for those kinds of daring deeds," she admitted shyly.

He seemed slightly disappointed, but became his chivalrous self again in the blink of an eye. "What would my lady prefer to do?"

"I'm not sure. Let's walk around and see the sights."

Richard bought her a roasted ear of corn and a candy apple. They went to the wild animal arena and viewed the tiger, lion, and other exotic animals. They listened to a band play and they gazed in wonder at the Electric Theatre. She had a pleasant time.

"It's been a delightful evening, Richard." She was hoping he would get the hint and offer to take her home.

"It's not over, yet. We must ride the Ferris wheel."

"Oh, I don't know." She strained her neck to look up at the giant wheel. "It's so high."

"I assure you, we will be quite safe."

"I'm not sure . . ."

"Let's be adventurous." He gave her a bright smile.

He took her by the elbow and urged her forward. Before she could utter another word in protest, they were sitting closely in the metal contraption. Her stomach dropped as the wheel groaned upward. She clasped her gloved hands in her lap and tried not to panic.

"Look." He pointed. "You can see the Santa Fe Depot from here."

She was afraid to move her head. She didn't want the seat to rock any more than it already was. She cut her eyes in that direction and muttered through clenched teeth, "Yes. I see."

"Rose, you really are frightened." He leaned toward her, reached out, took her hands in his and squeezed them.

She could have sworn she saw a hint of amusement cross his features. It made her angry enough to jerk her hands away from his. The basket swayed from her abrupt movements. She grasped the railing in front of her.

"I'm ready to go home," she ground out.

"Of course, my dear Rose. I did not intend to alarm you in any way."

He seemed sincere, but she was so irked she wasn't able to simmer down until the Ferris wheel made its final revolution. She didn't appreciate being coerced into doing anything.

She let him assist her out, but marched ahead of him. She made it all the way to his buggy before she turned around and found that he wasn't behind her. Now she was embarrassed. She had caused a scene and now she had to wait for him like a contrite child.

He soon arrived. He strolled toward her with his hands behind his back. He seemed truly remorseful.

"Richard, I—"

"Rose, I am mortified that I subjected you to such a trial." He brought a bouquet of multicolored carnations from behind his back and held them up for her. "You have my sincerest apologies."

How could she refuse such an acknowledgement of his actions?

"Thank you." She accepted the flowers.

"I should have realized some young ladies are more . . . delicate than others."

She sighed and wished he had stopped talking while he was ahead.

"Let me take you home. You appear done in."

"Yes. It's been a long day. I would appreciate that."

All sorts of goods continued to be dropped off the following day. Everything was to be hauled by train on Saturday and there was much to do to prepare for it. Rose was relieved to be extra busy to keep her mind off Richard. It was so difficult for her to sort out her feelings for him.

It was almost lunchtime when Betty popped her head into the back room.

"Rose. Mrs. Logan is here and would like to know if you're free for lunch?"

Rose raised her eyebrows at Owen.

He glanced at Hope who was sitting in the baby stroller sucking on a wooden rattle. He gave Rose a smile and a nod.

"Tell her I'll be right out," Rose informed Betty.

She removed her apron, tidied herself, put her hat on and went out to find Ada waiting at the front of the store.

"How are you, Rose?" Ada greeted her. "Luke took a harness down to Unzner's store to get it repaired. There's no telling how long he'll be there, so I thought you and I might have lunch together at the Norwood."

"That would be lovely."

Rose welcomed the walk as it eased her aching shoulders and back. They arrived at the Norwood hotel and went under the wrought-iron balcony. They entered the lobby and went inside to the restaurant at the left. They settled at a table beside a large plate glass window.

"As I recall, this is where we sat when we first made our acquaintance," Ada said. "I can hardly believe I've been here almost a year."

"So much has happened for you, hasn't it?"

"Yes, I quit acting, moved here, fell for and married

Luke. It's no wonder time went by so fast. But, this will be your year to fall in love. I feel it in my bones." She reached over and squeezed Rose's hand.

"I'm not so sure about that."

A waitress appeared at their table. They placed their orders and continued their conversation.

"You went to the carnival with Richard, didn't you?" Ada inquired.

"Yes." She could feel her face redden. "We had a nice time, but I'm just not sure about him."

"What do you mean?" She showed a look of concern.

"I haven't really decided how I feel about him, and then there's . . ."

"Owen?"

She nodded and leaned forward. "I don't know what to do, Ada. I have strong affections for Owen, but my mother likes Richard. He *is* rather charming, and he seems to have an attraction toward me."

"Charm isn't always a virtue."

"I know. Maybe that's what bothers me. Richard is almost pompous. I wonder if he's genuine at times. Plus, I have to be so prim and proper that I don't feel like I can be myself."

"How do you feel when you're with Owen?"

She gave her a shy smile. "He's so different. He's unpretentious. I feel a little nervous around him, but it's an exciting sort of emotion. At the same time, I'm comfortable around him. It seems at times like we've always known each other." She shook her head as all the sentiments that she had been restraining came tumbling out. "But, it's complicated with Owen. He's still mourning his wife. Will he ever have any regards for me? Should I fall in love with someone who may never return it or keep seeing someone who seems to admire me?"

Ada pondered her dilemma several moments. "I understand your plight. The answer seems obvious to me, but you should keep searching your heart and don't do anything rash."

"You aren't going to tell me which one I should choose?" She tried not to be dismayed.

"No. I think you'll soon know which one to put your hopes on."

"I keep trying to remind myself that God will help me know and give me peace about it, but it's not easy."

"I know what you mean." Ada's countenance became melancholy. "I've been struggling to have peace about something too."

"You have?" Rose was perplexed. Ada seemed to have a perfect existence.

Her normal confidence was replaced with a tinge of embarrassment. "I'm troubled that I'm not with child yet. Luke doesn't seem to be bothered by it, but what if it never happens? We both want a family so badly."

"You've only been married a few months." She tried to think of a way to encourage her.

"I know. I keep trying to tell myself that, but I'm not a very patient person. I'm used to deciding what I want and doing it. That frame of mind worked well as a businesswoman, but not so much now." She shook her head.

"Well, I can't believe it won't happen. It's not easy to wait, though, is it?"

"No." Her green eyes expressed the sadness she felt.

"Let's promise to pray for each other. Insight for me and children for you."

A brilliant smile crossed Ada's lips. "That sounds like a wonderful idea to me."

Chapter Fifteen

Owen closed the ledger book for the day. He couldn't quite believe they were already into the month of May. He checked that the front door was locked and made his way through the store, past the stockroom, and up the stairs.

He had a feeling something was wrong as soon as he opened the door. It was too quiet. Rose turned from the window where she was standing with Hope.

"She's sick, Owen," Rose told him as she came forward.

"Oh, no." His heart dropped and a sense of dread washed over him.

Hope's cheeks were pink and her nose was runny. Her eyes were droopy as she reached out for him. When he held her close, he could tell she was warmer than usual.

"She has a little bit of a fever," Rose said as she stroked Hope's head.

"What do I do? I don't know how to take care of a sick baby," he uttered helplessly.

He could see the tender compassion in her eyes as she gazed at him. "The only thing I know to do is not bundle her too much. Wiping her face and neck with a damp rag will help too."

He nodded, but still felt vulnerable.

"Will you let me fix you supper before I leave?"

"I'm not hungry," he muttered into Hope's hair.

"How about some eggs and fried ham? You'll need something. It might be a long night."

He assented.

"I'll telephone Mother and tell her I'll be late coming home." She hurried away.

He placed Hope on the floor long enough to remove his suit coat. She whimpered for him until he could pick her up.

"I'm sorry you're sick, Buttercup." He kissed her forehead, hating the heat he found there.

Rose returned and quickly whipped up a meal for him. He didn't have much appetite, but he dutifully ate while Rose sat with him. She gently sang to his baby.

"You'll be an excellent mother someday," he spoke without thinking. He could tell that he embarrassed her.

"I hope so," she replied quietly. "You're a good father, you know."

"I don't know about that." He took a drink of coffee.

"I feel like I'm flying by the seat of my pants most of the time."

"Well, you have wonderful instincts and you'll do fine."

He shrugged. He chased a bite of fried egg around his plate. He finally pushed his plate away. "Could you stay long enough for me to milk Nan?"

"Certainly."

"I'll get to it, then."

The chair scraped the floor as he stood. He went down to do his chores. Taking care of the goat had become second nature to him. If only a baby was so easy. He finished his job and trudged upstairs, already weary from worrying about the night ahead.

He let himself back in. Rose had Hope on her hip and was putting away the last spotless dish.

"I could have done that," he said.

"I didn't mind." A soft smile crossed her lips.

He walked to the table, strained the milk, and poured it into clean bottles. After washing everything, he reached for Hope.

"Thank you for staying awhile. You can go on. We'll be fine," he said, knowing he didn't sound very confident.

"Are you sure?" Concern was written all over her lovely face.

"Yes." He escorted her to the door. "We'll see you in the morning."

"Of course." She began to leave, but turned back. "I hope you two have a good night."

The sound of the shutting door seemed to echo through his home reminding him how alone he was. He wanted to chase Rose down and beg her to stay all night, but he knew that would never be proper. He thought about telephoning Betty to come over, but she didn't know any more about children than he did. He was on his own.

He held Hope to his cheek and closed his eyes. "I hope you'll be fine, Buttercup. I hope I'll know how to help you."

Hope relaxed and snuggled against him, something she rarely did. Her simple gesture made him feel better and not quite so desperate. He went to get her a bottle. He could only do what he knew and take it one moment at a time. They settled into the rocking chair. He was ready for the evening to begin.

Rose fretted about Hope and Owen most of the night. The next morning, she could not stop herself from going to work early to check on them. She knocked lightly on Owen's door. When there was no response, she tried the knob and it turned.

She peeked in, hoping Owen wasn't indisposed or she would embarrass them both. She quickly saw that he was lying propped up on the couch in the clothes he wore the previous day. Hope was dozing on his chest; his arms were cradling her as he slept. She crept toward them. Her heart gave a little skip as she watched them together. She had never witnessed such a tender moment.

"Owen?" she spoke quietly, hoping she wouldn't startle him.

He jerked slightly, his hands grasping Hope as his eyes snapped open. "Rose?" He looked confused for a second. "Is it morning?"

"Yes." She touched Hope's face. "She doesn't seem as warm today. How was last night?"

He was bedraggled as he pushed himself into a sitting position and laid Hope down into his arms without waking her. He ran his fingers through his wayward hair.

"It wasn't too bad. She didn't want me to put her down, though. She'd wake up every time. She breathed funny when she was laying flat too. Once we were upright, she slept better." He looked down at Hope and stroked her red, sleep-wrinkled cheek. "I should probably go clean up. I'll see if I can lay her down."

He stood slowly and carefully walked over to Hope's cradle and put her down. She stirred, but didn't awaken. He left her and returned to Rose.

"If you'll excuse me, I'll do the milking and get ready."

"Of course. Would you like some breakfast?"

He glanced at the nickel-plated alarm clock on the chiffonier. "I don't really have time."

"At least some bread and jam?"

"Yes. Thank you. I'll be back in a few minutes." He rushed away.

Rose went to the kitchen cabinet, removed the lid off

the decorated tin bread box and took out a golden loaf of bakery bread. She found a knife and cut two thick slices. She opened a jar of apricot preserves and slathered it on the bread. She placed them on a plate and set the table. She hoped he would sit and take a moment to eat.

It wasn't long before he returned. She took care of the goat's milk while he went into the bathroom to freshen up. When he came out, he smelled of soap and pomade and seemed to be fortified for the day ahead. He sat down and ate his breakfast quickly. After he swallowed the last drop of milk, he wiped his mouth with a napkin.

"Thank you, Rose," he said with a smile. He stood and laid his napkin on the table. "I'll take a look at Hope before I go."

As he went toward the cradle, Rose decided to follow him. She stood behind him and peered over his shoulder as he bent and lightly placed his hand on Hope's rising belly.

She turned her attention back to him when she noticed his collar was damp. Her eyes trailed to the back of his head. He had gone to the barber the previous day at lunchtime and there was a thin horizontal line of pale skin where the hair had been trimmed on his neck. His skin looked so soft. She had to fight the urge to touch him.

It was then that she realized she loved him. She loved Owen Emerson to the tips of her toes.

She was taken aback when he turned around. She

stumbled. He reached out and caught her, bringing her close to his body to steady her.

"I didn't mean to knock you over." He grinned.

"I . . . It was my fault . . . ," she stammered. Her heart was beating so hard she was afraid he could hear it.

He looked at her intently. His lips parted as if to say something, but instead he released her self-consciously. He ducked his head and brushed past her.

"I'd better get to work," he stated without looking back.

She stood there knowing that whether it was prudent or not, she wanted him and no other. She would have to tell Richard she didn't wish to see him anymore. She dreaded it with every bone in her body.

She didn't get the chance to have that talk with Richard until after chorus practice Saturday. She invited him to join her on the front porch. She knew she was being impolite by not offering him some refreshment, but she didn't want to postpone her odious task any longer.

She settled onto the porch swing, and he casually took his place beside her.

"I'm glad we have this moment to ourselves, Rose." He took her hands into his. "I've wanted to tell you of my undying admiration—"

"Stop, Richard." Panic filled her voice. She pulled her hands away.

"I think you should know how I feel." His eyebrows were knit together.

"But, I need to tell you something."

"Let me say it first, my dear. I love—"

"No!" She jumped up and almost dumped him onto the floor. "No, Richard. Don't say it." She wrung her hands as she stood before him. "I . . . I'm sorry, Richard, but I don't wish to see you anymore," she said quickly.

"You don't wish to see me anymore?" He seemed dazed as he tried to process what she said.

"I do apologize."

"You apologize?" He stood slowly and deliberately. He towered over her. "After all the rides, money frittered away, and time spent at that infernal singing practice? You can*not* be serious."

"But, I am." She cringed inwardly from the confrontation.

He was clearly angry. He clenched his fists and glanced at the house where her mother was waiting. He glowered at Rose and moved so close she could feel his hot breath on her face. "It's Emerson and that brat, isn't it? Why should he get your inheritance? He's no better than me."

"Inheritance? I don't have any inheritance." She was dumfounded.

"I heard you and Gwen talking about it at the mercantile before I met you."

"She was only teasing. Mother had bills to pay after

Father died. We only have enough money to get by on," she rushed to explain.

Her words seemed to only infuriate him more. He cursed and roughly grabbed her face. He crushed her lips with his. He pulled back slightly, his hands still squeezing her cheeks.

"I've waited far too long for that," he ground out through clenched teeth. "Good-bye it is. But, be assured, I will not be made a fool."

He stomped down the steps. He glared at her one last time before he climbed into his buggy. He yanked out a whip and slapped the back of his horse before it bounded off.

Rose was trembling. She had never been handled in such a harsh way before. She was terribly unnerved, but she was also ashamed. She thought she should have told him sooner, maybe he wouldn't have been so hateful.

She let herself in and quietly shut the door behind her. She hoped to sneak upstairs so she could regain her composure.

"There you are," her mother said as she came from the kitchen carrying a tray with a teapot and two teacups. "Where is Richard?"

"He's gone."

"Honestly, Rose, your manners are atrocious. You should have invited the poor man in." She stepped to the kitchen table and put the tray down. She turned back to her. "Did he say why he had to leave so soon?"

"He left because I told him I didn't want to see him

anymore," she said quietly as she stared at the braided rag rug on the floor.

"Are you serious? He was a perfectly nice suitor."

"I know, but . . ."

Her mother put her hands on her hips. "Your father and I tried our hardest to find a suitable husband for you and you never showed any interest. Richard has been courting you for months and you toss him aside? Why in the world would you do that?"

"After I got to know him, he didn't seem authentic."

"Authentic? What it that supposed to mean?"

"He's not as genuine and nice as he appears."

"Hmm."

She could tell her mother was trying to assimilate all the information. Rose decided she might as well tell her the entire truth while she was at it. "That was one reason. The other is because I love someone else."

"You do?" Her eyebrows lifted. "Who?"

"It's Owen."

"Owen?"

"Yes."

"Are you prepared to be an instant mother?"

"I think so. I'm already taking care of her most of the time," Rose said.

"It's not the same." Her mother paused. "Are you certain?"

"I truly believe they're in my life for a reason."

She seemed to reconcile herself with it. "Does he return the sentiments?"

"I think he's still in mourning, but I'm prepared to wait."

"It might not be easy, my dear." She came forward and put a wisp of hair behind her ear.

"I know."

She kissed her cheek. "All I ever want is your happiness. I hope you'll have it soon."

Chapter Sixteen

With her newfound revelations about Owen, every moment with him was something Rose wanted to memorize. She found herself watching his every move when they were together. When she was alone, she would recall the sincerity of his smiles, the depth of his voice, or the strength of his hands as he performed a task.

On the opposite spectrum, Richard seemed to be out of her life. He stopped coming to choir practice and church, but she did occasionally see him around town. She was grateful she didn't have to be around him much.

The pleasant weather of May turned into the sweltering days of June. One Sunday afternoon, Rose was in the yard at the rear of the house cutting roses to take in. Her two-and-half-year-old neighbor, Henry, came flying out of his screen door carrying something big and

139

black. The door barely had time to slam before Aletha raced out.

"Come back here, Henry!" she demanded.

Henry laughed and chanted, "No, no, no."

She chased him around the yard and had almost caught him when he stopped in his tracks, threw his possession down, and sat on it.

"Oh, Henry! No," she exclaimed. She pulled him up and picked up the smashed object. "This is my only hat," she said forlornly. She stood examining the hat that seemed beyond repair.

Rose came out from around the bushes and said, "Aletha."

Aletha picked up Henry and came over to the fence.

"I have an extra hat if you'd like it. I bought a new one a while back, but my old one was perfectly good. I'd love for you to get some use out of it."

"Well . . ." Her neighbor glanced at the damaged one in her hand. "I don't like taking charity, but I can't afford another right now . . ."

"Just think of it as one friend giving another a little gift."

She nodded. A smile crossed her tired face. "Thank you, Rose."

One evening, near closing time, Owen was checking the inventory of gold rings as Gwen swept in and came directly toward him.

"How are you today?" he asked with a grin.

"Wonderful." She held up a picnic basket. "Rose and I are having a picnic in the park. I must be early for a change." Her eyes twinkled.

He began to put the velvet lined tray away.

"Wait. I'd like to look at those."

She was marveling at all the rings when Rose and Hope came up to them.

"Look at these, Rose. I like this one and this one." She pointed.

"Yes, and I always admired that one." She motioned to a flat band with vines and flowers and small diamond with rubies on either side.

Gwen picked it up and put it on Rose's fourth finger. "It even fits. It looks like it was made for you, Rose."

"Oh . . . well . . . Are you ready to go?" Her cheeks turned the darkest shade of pink.

"Of course." Gwen removed the ring and gave it back to Owen.

He replaced the tray, knowing he would always remember which ring Rose preferred.

"I almost forgot." Gwen smacked her forehead. "I wanted to remind the two of you about the ball at the Norwood on July fourth. Walter promised to come, and we'll all have a grand time."

"I don't know—" He tried not to squirm.

"I'm not sure." Rose appeared uncomfortable also.

"Come on. Don't disappoint me. Ada and Luke are going. Let's go together. Please. It will be so much fun."

There was a long pause before Owen finally said, "I'll think about it."

"I hope you will." Gwen said amiably before she turned to Rose. "I'm ready if you are."

Rose handed Hope to him, and he watched them leave the store. What would he do? Would he be bold enough to ask Rose to the dance? It was apparent that Gwen expected him to.

That Dobbs fellow must not be in the picture anymore or he would have surely asked Rose already. He hadn't seen him around lately. He had to admit he was more than glad to not see him hovering over Rose at church.

Where did that leave him? Did he care for Rose? Of course. Was he attracted to her? Definitely. Would he court her to see how their friendship would develop? He wasn't sure.

He sighed. He would have to ponder over it some more and decide if it was worth the risk to his heart.

Rose and Gwen sat on a bench at Woodland Park with the picnic basket between them. Gwen opened it and handed Rose a sandwich wrapped in paper.

"I believe you're as fond of bacon sandwiches as I am."

"Yes. It sounds delicious."

"And, I talked Mrs. Brown into letting me have two big slices of her famous rum cake."

"You'll have to thank her for me." She smiled.

"Oh, I will. I don't think she would have relinquished

any if I hadn't said it was for you too." Gwen unwrapped her sandwich. "She told me that if that sweet, angelic Miss Dennis likes her cake then she shall have a piece." She chuckled.

"Do people really see me that way?" Rose was curious.

"You *are* considered unequaled. You're so flawless, you make the rest of us look bad," she joked, and then took a crunchy bite.

"I don't know why anyone would think I'm perfect," she fumed, putting her food on her lap. "I get angry. It irritates me that Owen looks at me with what seems like longing, but won't act on it. I'm jealous. I can stand the fact that he had a life with another girl and she's probably what is in the way of my happiness. I get afraid too. The only thing I ever wanted in life was a man to love me as much as I love him and raise a family. I'm scared sometimes it will never happen." Her fury dwindled to uncertainty.

"I'm sorry, Rose." Gwen used her free hand, leaned over and gave her shoulders a squeeze. "I know we all have our trials. I take it that things haven't changed with Owen, then?"

"No. He's as friendly as usual. Sometimes I think I see a little spark in his eyes when he talks to me. But, I don't know." She shrugged. "And, he hasn't even noticed my new hat, yet." She knew it sounded silly, but she couldn't help being miffed that he wouldn't or couldn't notice.

"Maybe he has been preoccupied."

"Maybe. I was hoping since Richard wasn't around anymore, things might progress with Owen. Nothing is different so far." She fingered the paper on her sandwich.

"Well, I tried to help today." Gwen smiled. "I was hoping you wouldn't think it too forward of me to encourage him to come with us to the ball. I thought maybe if he felt like it was an evening out with friends, he might come and then he'd be so captivated by your beauty that he would be yours forever," she said dreamily.

Rose's mood began to brighten. "It didn't seem to work."

"Well, don't give up yet. Do you have a dress to wear in case he comes around at the last minute?"

"I thought I might wear that black gown that Ada gave me last year. It's the nicest one I own."

"You did look stunning in it," Gwen agreed as she nodded. "If Owen sees you in that dress, he won't have a chance."

For several days, Owen questioned whether he should invite Rose to the ball or not. Part of him wanted to do it; the other part of him thought it was too soon. He was tired of being indecisive, though, and knew he must put the matter to rest.

One evening, he opened the door and found Rose humming and dancing with Hope. Her movements were fluid as she swayed in time. Even her shadow on the floor was graceful. She twirled around and spotted him.

"Oh, hello." She smiled shyly. "She was a little fussy, so I thought a song would help."

"Is she sick?" He walked toward them.

"No, I think a tooth is coming in. You can feel a bump on her bottom gums."

"That's a relief." He ruffled Hope's ever growing curls.

His eyes went back to Rose. The light from the window produced a radiance about her. She was wearing a light pink walking skirt and a pristine white lawn shirtwaist. His gaze traveled along the elegant curve of her neck up to the soft outline of her cheek that was turning brighter the longer he stared. He finally knew. He wanted her in his life.

"Rose . . ."

"Yes?" She looked at him expectantly.

He took a deep breath. It had been so long since he'd done this. "Has anyone asked to escort you to the Independence Day Ball?"

"No."

"I thought maybe that Dobbs fellow might have already." He fidgeted with the button on his jacket sleeve.

"No . . . I told him that I didn't wish to see him anymore."

"You did?" He couldn't believe how happy that made him.

"Yes. I did." Her lips turned up slightly.

"I . . . I was wondering if you would like to go to the ball with me?"

"I would enjoy that."

He thought he should make his intentions clear. "I'm not a rich man, but I'm a hard worker. I've been married and I have a child. I'm not sure if I've finished grieving, and I'm not sure I'm good enough for you, but I would like to court you." He finally stopped blathering.

"I would like that too." She reached out and tentatively touched his sleeve.

He placed a hand over hers. His heart was thudding from his speech and the nearness of her.

Suddenly, Hope leaned over and batted his cheek with her little palm. That movement ended his moment with Rose. He took his baby from her.

"I should go," Rose said quietly. She brushed past him and went to the coat rack to retrieve her hat. She settled it onto her head and stuck the pin through.

She put her hand on the doorknob, but turned back. "Would you and Hope like to join my mother and me for lunch on Sunday?"

"That sounds terrific."

"Good. I'll see you then."

"Good-bye." He watched her open the door. "And, Rose?"

She paused.

"You look pretty in your new hat."

Rose beamed with delight, waved, and swept out the door.

Chapter Seventeen

Owen arrived at Rose's house in Bob's borrowed rig. Rose seemed pleased when she opened the door and eagerly ushered them in. She captured Hope right away and led them into the kitchen.

"You're right on time," she informed him.

Mrs. Dennis was ladling steaming liquid into a gravy boat. She turned to him. In spite of the heat emitting from the kitchen, she appeared as cool and fresh as her daughter. Her smile was polite but not overly friendly.

"Welcome, Mr. Emerson."

"Thank you for having us over, ma'am. Please call me Owen."

She nodded and said, "Follow me, Owen. We're ready."

She led the way into a small dining room. The table

147

was set with fine silverware and china. A huge vase of pink, white, red, and yellow roses sat in the center. A woman's touch was evident in every detail.

It hadn't been in Amanda's nature to fuss about those kinds of things when they lived in a boardinghouse. He couldn't remember when someone had taken such care over him. It must have been nearly nine years. It was before his mother died.

Rose placed Hope on the floor in the corner. "Here's my old rag dolly, Hope. Do you want to play with it while we eat?"

Chubby Hope sat and examined the doll. Before long it was in her mouth.

He helped Rose and her mother into their seats and then took his own. He picked up the starched white linen napkin and placed it on his lap. The food looked wonderful. There was a roasted chicken, mashed potatoes, gravy, green peas, and sliced cucumbers and onions soaked in vinegar water.

They began their meal with prayer. He tried not to make a pig out of himself, but the food was delicious. He was taking a second delicate yeast roll out of the basket that Rose was offering, when Hope decided she had been still long enough. She leaned over with her hands on the floor and rocked back and forth and propelled herself forward with feet, hands and knees.

"She did it!" he announced without thinking.

"She did!" Rose clapped her hands with glee.

Hope continued forward until she came to Mrs.

Dennis' skirts. Owen began to rise, but Mrs. Dennis waved him back. She reached down and picked her up.

"Did you just accomplish something, my dear?" Mrs. Dennis asked with a lilting voice.

Hope babbled back to her.

"I'll take her if you'd like, Mother," Rose offered.

"No, she is fine right here." She placed Hope on her lap, and Hope played with a teaspoon while Mrs. Dennis continued to eat.

"So, Owen, how long were you married to this little darling's mother?" Mrs. Dennis asked.

"Amanda and I were married about nine months."

"Newlyweds. How unfortunate. Did you two court for long?"

He knew he was being scrutinized. He wanted to answer her questions well. "Not long, Mrs. Dennis. We married quickly. We had both lost our parents and were ready to be a family." He paused. "I don't tend to act hastily. I'd like Hope to have a mother, but I'm not going to rush to find one for her. I want a compatible, happy marriage. Without that, she couldn't have the right mother."

Mrs. Dennis studied him for a moment before a genuine smile crossed her lips. "That is commendable in your situation, Owen."

"Thank you, ma'am." He glanced at Rose, who seemed happy with his answers.

Except for Hope banging her spoon on the table, they finished their meal in companionable silence.

"Why don't the two of you enjoy the outdoors before it becomes too warm?" Mrs. Dennis asked. "I'll see if Hope would like some smashed peas if that's agreeable to you?"

"Yes. Thank you."

He pulled Rose's chair out and followed her to the back door and opened it for them. They walked around the yard, enjoying the flower garden. The air was humid and heavy with the scent of roses. When they came to an arbor of white roses, she sat down and motioned for him to join her. Bees hummed as they continued their work undisturbed.

"I apologize if my mother made you uncomfortable with her questions," she said.

"Believe me, I understand. She's only looking out for her daughter." He smiled. "Make sure she knows how much I appreciate the effort you two made for me today. I haven't been surrounded by such fine things since my mother died."

"I'll tell her, but we were happy to do it." Her eyes held his. "Do you still have anything that belonged to your mother?"

"I do. The only thing I found when I went through the ashes that wasn't ruined or broken was her favorite crystal vase. It's about eight inches tall and has etched butterflies on it. She would keep fresh cut flowers in it all summer long. I think it's in the back of the kitchen cabinet," he paused. "I started a butterfly collection because of that vase."

"I love butterflies too. They're so delicate as they flit around and yet durable enough to withstand summer storms." She pointed to a large yellow-and-black striped one that was sitting on a pink zinnia nearby sunning its wings. "What is that one? I've seen them before and think they're just beautiful."

He leaned forward and studied it to be sure. "It's a tiger swallowtail. That's a fine specimen. The one I had was smaller than that one." He gestured to a tiny silver blue butterfly fluttering near a small purple wildflower at their feet. "That's an eastern tailed blue hairstreak. Can you see the tiny tails coming from their back wings? They look like hairs."

"Oh, they do. I never noticed them before."

"I must be boring you." He paused awkwardly. "I could tell it made Amanda weary to listen to me speak of insects for long."

"No, Owen. I truly do think it's interesting. I've always enjoyed learning, especially about nature," she said earnestly.

He nodded. He was overwhelmed by her sincerity. He picked up her pale velvety hand. Her fingers were long and thin. They were strong yet feminine. He put her knuckles to his lips, then turned her hand over and placed a kiss in her palm.

"Thanks for being you," he murmured against her skin.

Despite the heat of the summer day, he could feel her shiver. She cupped his cheek with her hand and rubbed her thumb along his cheekbone.

He couldn't take his eyes off of her. Her irises were of the deepest blue and the most expressive he had ever seen. The admiration he saw there energized and scared him out of his wits at the same time.

He exhaled slowly. "I suppose we should go in and see how your mother is faring with Hope."

"I suppose we should," she agreed.

They stood in unison. She rested her forearm in the crook of his elbow and leaned into him as they ambled toward the house. When they entered, they found Mrs. Dennis cleaning up in the kitchen with Hope playing with a couple of small cooking pots and lids.

"I'll help you, Mother," Rose offered.

"No, we're fine, dear. Why don't you play something? I imagine we would all enjoy it," she said over her shoulder as she scrubbed a dish.

"Yes. I would love to hear you," he agreed.

Rose smiled a smile that was meant only for him and he followed her into the parlor. He sat in a nearby burgundy chair while she took a piece of music out of the bench. She apparently knew right away which one she wanted because she didn't flip through the large stack.

She settled at the piano, arranged the sheets, and touched the keys. She began playing quietly and slowly building up to a fiery intensity. She swayed with the flow of the music. He could see the side of her face and her countenance was pure bliss as she completed the few final quiet notes.

They both remained as they were for several moments. He was the first to move. She looked up at him as he went to her. He wished he could capture the expression on her upturned face. He wanted to remember it forever. He reached out and slid his fingers around the side of her neck, into the fine strands of her hair and stroked his thumb along the silky area near her ear.

"What song was that?" he asked quietly.

" 'Lovedream' " she whispered.

"This does seem like a dream, doesn't it?" he muttered. "The music was almost as beautiful as you."

He wanted to kiss her. He bent down. He searched her eyes and saw the willingness there. His lips were a hairsbreadth away from hers.

"That was lovely, dear," Mrs. Dennis commented as she came from the kitchen.

Owen jumped back as if he had touched fire. He was sure he looked as guilty as he felt.

Mrs. Dennis eyed them as if she suspected something, but was still polite. "I think your darling Hope is ready for a nap."

"Yes. It's about time." He held out his arms and took Hope from her. "We'll take our leave. Thank you so much, Mrs. Dennis. The food . . . everything was wonderful."

"It was our pleasure, Owen. We will have the two of you back again soon," Mrs. Dennis replied.

"I'll see you tomorrow, Rose."

"Yes." She grinned.

"Good-bye, then." He opened the door and exited as quickly as he could.

Rose closed the door behind Owen and Hope. The splendid afternoon together ended too soon for her. She twirled around, humming the melody she had just played.

Her mother stood with her arms crossed. She was clearly displeased.

"What is it, Mother?" she asked although she was certain she knew what was wrong.

"It appeared I interrupted a moment between the two of you."

"Well . . . not exactly . . ." She wasn't sure how to appease her.

"I do remember what it's like to be young and courting, Rose. While I know it will take time before any understanding can be reached between the two of you, I don't think it is prudent to be unchaperoned around him."

"Of course, Mother." She hated that her mother felt like she couldn't trust them.

"I don't think you should work for him any longer."

"What?" Her heart dropped. "No, Mother, I can't quit. He needs me. Hope needs me."

"You are of age and I know I cannot stop you—"

"I assure you nothing inappropriate has ever happened. He truly is a gentleman."

"He may be a gentleman, but he has also been a *married* man. He knows—"

"Mother, please. You have my word. I would never do anything to be ashamed of."

Her mother uncrossed her arms and wearily rubbed her temple.

"Hope is always there and Bob and Betty are almost always downstairs." She made one last effort to change her mind.

"I don't know, Rose." She was still wary.

"I promise, Mother." She clasped her hands to her chest. "Please, tell me you don't mind if I stay on."

Her mother finally assented. "You can continue for *now.*"

Chapter Eighteen

Rose knocked on Owen's door with an armload of flowers that she had cut at first light.

He opened the door and let her in. He glanced at her bounty and asked, "Flowers?"

"They're to put in your mother's vase."

"Ah, Rose. That's so thoughtful of you." He reached out and touched her arm.

A little shiver ran up her arm and down her spine from his simple gesture.

"I think the vase is in the cabinet behind everything. If you want to do that, I'll change Hope out of her nightdress."

"That sounds good." She laid her load on the table and rummaged through the dishes and canisters until she found it. The clear vase was sturdy at the base and it became thinner and more delicate as it sloped outward to the scalloped rim. Several butterflies and roses were engraved into the crystal. It was lovely. She filled it with water and artfully arranged the colorful roses, daisies, and zinnias.

By the time she had finished her task, Owen had completed his. He and Hope joined her in the kitchen area.

"Rose," he said softly. He looked at the flowers in the center of the table.

They stood silently side by side. She felt his sinewy fingers find hers in the folds of her skirt. He clasped her hand momentarily and let go too soon.

He faced her. His eyes were misty as he whispered, "Thank you."

"You're welcome. I just . . . I wanted to bring you some memories of your mother and to brighten your day."

"You have."

Rose became more excited as each day before the ball passed. She could hardly wait for the festive atmosphere, the orchestral music, and the dancing. The thought of dancing with Owen and being so near him made her weak in the knees.

She was still daydreaming about it all on the third of July when Owen came up early to ask if she could help watch the store. Betty had to run to the butcher down on East Main, Bob needed to take his horse to the livery to have Mr. Carey look at its lame foreleg, and Owen was trying to get some dishes unpacked from the crates in the stockroom.

As they landed at the bottom of the stairs, Owen paused and said, "It looks like I won't be able to borrow Bob's buggy tomorrow night."

"That's fine."

"Would you prefer to go with Gwen and the others?"

"No. Let's meet somewhere before we see everyone else," she suggested.

"That sounds good," he paused thoughtfully. "How about on the balcony of the Norwood at about nine o'clock?"

"Yes, I'd like that." She smiled.

The bell rang in the front of the mercantile as a customer entered.

"I'll take care of them," she informed him. She left him behind and carried Hope with her through the doorway into the store.

A young woman was standing near the register, looking around uncertainly. She had removed her hat and was nervously turning it around in her hands. Her blue traveling dress appeared new and modern, but her blond hair was done up in an old-fashioned way with a long braid encircling the top of her head. Rose noticed the pleasant features of her face as she turned toward her.

"May I help you, Miss?" Rose asked.

"This is where Mr. Owen Emerson works?" she asked with a detectable Swedish accent.

"Yes. He's occupied at the moment. May I assist you?"

"My name is Ingrid Sorenson. I just arrived on the train from Wichita. Owen is a . . . close friend of mine."

A close friend? How intimate of friends must they be for her to travel so far to see him?

"Is this Hope?" Miss Sorenson asked as she came forward. "It is. My, how my little precious one has grown," she cooed as she touched Hope's chubby hand. "May I hold her? It's been so long since she's been in my arms."

"Well, I'm not sure . . ."

"Rose?" Owen's voice preceded him as he emerged from the back. "I was wondering—"

He stopped in his tracks. His face blanched as if he'd seen a ghost. "Ingrid," he said hoarsely.

"Hello, Owen," Miss Sorenson greeted.

He came forward as if in a daze. He took Hope and held her to his chest. Without taking his eyes off of Miss Sorenson, he said, "Rose, I believe we'll close early today. I'll see you tomorrow."

She had been dismissed without any mindfulness on Owen's part. To say she was hurt was an understatement. She hurried out the front door without looking back.

Owen finally came out of the shock of seeing Ingrid and locked the door after Rose left.

"Ingrid. Why are you here?" he asked.

"I came to see Hope . . . and you." She smiled tentatively.

"Well . . . I'm not sure why—"

"I've come this far." She nodded decisively as she spoke to herself. "I've come to talk you into your senses, Owen Emerson. You should come back to your home. Let me take care of Hope and you."

"Ingrid, I—"

"Please, hear me out." She held a hand up. "Amanda asked me on her deathbed to watch over the two of you. I promised I would. I had hoped you would forget about your plans to come to this godforsaken Territory, but you didn't. I let you go, assuming you would be back after you realized your folly. When your letters stopped coming to me, I decided it was time to bring you back." She seemed relieved that she had finished her speech.

"I don't know what to say." He was flabbergasted.

She stepped closer to him and placed her hat on the counter. She put one hand on his arm and the other on Hope's back. "I am Hope's godmother, but I would like to be her mother. We are friends. Marriages have begun with less."

He moved back. His mind was spinning. "I'm sorry, Ingrid."

"Sorry? Sorry about what?" Her face was more determined that ever. "Sorry that you made me wait and hope all these months?"

"Ingrid. I . . ." He tried to collect his thoughts. "I apologize if there has been some misunderstanding. I do appreciate your help when Hope was born. I know

I couldn't have done it without you, but I have a new life here."

"Then I will leave Mama and—"

"You don't understand. I'm courting someone," he said bluntly.

"Courting? Amanda isn't even nine months in her grave! It's one thing to marry a friend to help mother your child, but to woo someone so soon is a disgrace." She put her hands on her hips.

The compassion he had felt for her in the beginning was melting away. She was beginning to get his dander up. He remembered how Amanda loved Ingrid like a sister, but she had also thought Ingrid was overbearing at times. He was seeing that attitude all too clearly now.

"You have nothing to say?" Her eyes bored into his.

"No. I don't."

"Mama was right. I should have saved my money and my time. I will be Hope's godmother, but I will not trouble you again on this matter, Owen Emerson."

"Thank you. Have a safe trip back to Wichita." He tried to be nice.

She gave an unladylike snort before she said, *"Ja."*

She grabbed her hat and stomped away, but had to wait indignantly while he unlocked the door. He watched her skirts sway furiously as she marched away, head held high.

"Whew." He kissed Hope's forehead. "I think

we dodged a bullet on that one. We like Rose better, don't we?"

He could have sworn he heard Hope babble, *"Ja."*

Rose was exhausted when she awoke from a fitful night of sleep. Who was Ingrid Sorenson? Why did Owen shut himself up in a deserted store with this woman while calmly sending her away? Why hadn't he come or called to explain it all? She prided herself on being the kind of person who didn't jump to conclusions, but she was truly worried about the situation.

She had previously arranged to have the day off to watch the Independence Day parade with her friends. She decided to go on with them and hoped it would keep her mind off Owen and that other woman. She met up with Gwen and her fiancé, Walter, at the crowded corner of Market and Main streets just before the parade was to start.

"I was beginning to wonder about you," Gwen greeted her with a hug. "You remember Walter?" she asked.

He was as she remembered. He was tall and broad shouldered and had a square face. He bowed slightly, touched the rim of the black bowler hat in salutation, gave her a small smile and returned to his normal distinguished posture before he said, "A pleasure, Miss Dennis."

"Yes, it's nice to see you again."

"Are you ready for the ball tonight?" Gwen asked, her face was aglow with excitement.

"I'm not sure if I'm still going."

Walter politely turned toward the street to give them privacy.

"What? What's happened?" She leaned over to hear.

"A woman came from Wichita to see him yesterday. He . . . he asked me to leave without any explanation." She tried not to sound overly dramatic.

"Surely, it was nothing," Gwen insisted.

"I don't know. She seemed awfully possessive." She shrugged. "I don't know if he still wants to go with me or not."

"Have you asked him about it?"

"No. I thought he would tell me who she was."

"What are you going to do about tonight?" Gwen asked.

"I don't know." She sighed.

She let the subject drop, assuming it was over as the parade made its way toward them. The procession was led by Chief Sims on a white steed followed by a detail of police on horses.

"I'll be back in just a minute," Gwen said suddenly. She left the two of them gaping after her as she dashed across the street in front of the horses to the sidewalk on the other side.

"What in the world is she doing?" Walter exclaimed.

"I think she's coming to my rescue."

"Of course she is." He emitted a long suffering breath of weariness.

Owen took Hope out into the sunshine to join the crowds as they watched the parade. He had assumed

Rose would meet him to enjoy it together, but he hadn't seen any sign of her.

The large uniformed marching band had passed. A float with forty-six young ladies in white who were representing the states of the union was just going by when he saw Gwen dodging bystanders as she hurried through the throng.

"Owen," she said as she tried to catch her breath. "I can't stay for long, but I came to clear up a misunderstanding."

"What would that be?"

"Rose said a woman from your past came and now she's unsure if you still want to go to the ball with her."

"Of course I do." He recalled his reaction to Ingrid and his treatment of Rose. He was appalled that he had acted so callously. "Please, assure her that Ingrid was only an old friend and that she has gone back to Wichita. I'll explain everything tonight, if she'll meet me as planned," he implored.

"I thought it had to be something like that." She grinned. "I'd better get back. I'll see you later."

She turned, waved, and disappeared before he could count to ten.

Chapter Nineteen

Rose was ready. She stepped in front of her mirror to survey her appearance. She was surprised to find a pretty, confident young woman staring back. She had no qualms about meeting Owen. She knew he would tell her the truth. Everything would be settled and they would have a glorious evening.

She moved back to see her entire dress. The tiny black jet beads that dotted the midnight taffeta gown rattled softly with her movement. The small downy black feathers that encircled the low neckline and cap sleeves fluttered against her skin.

Ada had been more than generous the previous October to let her wear the gown to the last ball. Rose had been dumfounded when Ada insisted she keep it, saying it would never look as lovely as it did on her. She had never owned something so costly or so elegant.

She tucked a single black ostrich feather in her up-swept hair and was securing it with a pin when memories of the last time she wore the dress came flooding back. It had been a masquerade ball. She had danced almost the entire evening with one young man. She had worn a handmade mask and he had worn a store-bought lion mask. Their conversation had been light, and they had promised to reveal their identities at midnight with the other revelers, but he had received an urgent telegram and had to leave before she could find out who he was.

She had fancied at the time that he was the mysterious true love of her life, but she knew that was silly. Owen was the perfect one for her. He was flesh and blood. He was real and not some girlish fantasy. She shivered with anticipation.

She picked up her black elbow-length satin gloves and nearly floated out of her bedroom to meet Owen.

Owen paced along the wrought-iron railing on the second-story balcony of the Norwood Hotel in seclusion from the rest of the attendees. He kept glancing at the open French doors under the archway. Maybe he had dressed in his best frock coat for nothing.

He hoped he hadn't ruined his chance with Rose because of Ingrid. He had been frustrated that Ingrid had came, but, in hindsight, he was also glad she had. Seeing her and thinking about the past helped him finally put

Amanda aside. He had loved her as well as he could, but his marriage with her was in the past. He was ready now for a future with Rose.

Rose. The first time he had seen her he had been drawn to her like a moth to a flame. Her alabaster skin had fairly glowed in that black dress and even though he hadn't seen her face he had been intrigued by her gentle demeanor. Being married at the time, he knew he was playing with fire dancing with her so many times. He couldn't help feeling, though, that all he had been through somehow led to this moment.

He wondered if Rose would be angry or would his quick explanation to Gwen have squashed any negative feelings? Would she be as stirred with emotions as he was or would she be frightened by them? Would she come at all?

He thought he heard something. He stood still, trying to listen over the thundering of his heartbeat. There were light footsteps in the hallway. Rose emerged and seemed to glide before him. She paused in the doorway wearing that black dress.

"I wasn't sure if you would come," he finally found his voice.

"I wasn't either until Gwen talked to you."

He held out his hand. "Will you let me explain?"

She placed a gloved hand in his. "Yes."

It was dusk, the streetlights were beginning to come on. He led her to a shadowy section of the balcony. He turned to her and grasped her trembling hands.

"I didn't realize when Ingrid came how badly I treated you. I was shocked to see her. She was Amanda's friend and later mine. She was the one who helped me when Hope was born. I would have been lost without her, but I knew I needed to move here. She had become too attached to us. She came to Shawnee to convince me to marry her."

Rose's eyebrows arched with surprise.

"I sent her away. And, along with her went any remaining sadness over Amanda." He ran his index finger along her silken cheek. "You fill my every thought now."

"I feel the same," she whispered.

He moved nearer. He was so close, their bodies were almost touching. "You're so exquisite." He murmured against her temple.

She closed her eyes and a tiny sigh escaped her parted lips. He was drowning and the only person who could keep him afloat was Rose. He clutched her as if his life depended on it. His mouth found hers, gently at first, but more intensely as he felt her melt into him.

He finally stopped long enough to mumble into her ear, "You're even more beautiful than the first time I saw you in that dress."

"What?" She pulled back to look at him better. Her expression was puzzled.

"At the ball last October. I was the one in the lion mask. The one you danced with." He smiled tenderly.

She froze. A range of emotions crossed her face.

Astonishment turned to delight then her features settled on something akin to horror.

"But, that was the date Hope was born." She yanked herself out of his arms. "You were married . . ."

"Yes, the telegram that came was from Ingrid telling me Amanda was giving birth," he explained.

"How could you?" she asked with disgust.

"It was only some harmless fun. I wouldn't have even gone to the ball if Betty hadn't insisted." He tried to justify his actions.

"Harmless? You . . . I . . . ," she stammered. She gave him a look of total desolation before picking up her skirts and dashing away.

"Rose, wait!" he shouted. He started to chase her, but a crowd of distinguished-looking men and women came out of the elevator and blocked his way.

He didn't know whether to go after her now or give her time to process her thoughts. He felt he should give her some time. He bent down and picked up the black feather that had fallen from her hair. The aroma of her perfume emitted from it. He would wait for now.

"I won't cry. I will not cry in public," Rose said to herself as she scurried down the stairs. She landed in the lobby with her dress shoes clattering on the hardwood floors. She made her way through the brightly attired crowd and burst out the front doors.

She crashed into the back of a gentleman and nearly knocked him down.

"What the blazes?" The man swore as he stumbled forward. He stood his full height and turned around.

Rose was dismayed to see Richard glaring back at her.

"I'm sorry, Richard."

"Leaving the festivities so soon?" He grabbed her gloved wrist, forcing her to stay and talk to him.

"I can't stay."

"Did something ruin your perfect evening?"

She squirmed under his scrutiny and tried to wrench her arm away.

"Did you find out your knight was a cad after all?" He smirked.

"I . . ." She couldn't think of anything to say. She certainly wasn't going to tell him the truth.

He leaned down, his face inches from hers. "Was he too forward tonight? Did he hold you too tightly on the dance floor? Did he breathe on your lovely white neck?"

He reeked of alcohol. She knew she needed to get away from him.

"Or was the opposite true? Was he too meek and mild for you?"

"Richard!" she said through clenched teeth. Her arm was beginning to hurt as she tried to get loose.

"If he's not man enough for you, I'll be what you need," he said crudely.

"No. Stop!" she hissed.

"Rose," Gwen's voice came up behind her. "I've been looking for you."

Richard finally released her. "That's the last time you

refuse me," he threatened before turning on his heel and walking casually away.

"What's wrong?" Gwen steered her to a nearby alley.

"I can't tell you right now," she said willing tears back. "I can't face Owen tomorrow. Promise me you'll take care of Hope for me?"

"Well, I guess I can. Walter is going back in the morning." She seemed confused, but was willing to help out.

"Thank you." She moved away. "I have to go. I have to go!" she exclaimed.

She was free. She ran from the humiliation, knowing people were staring. Tears started flowing as she neared the park where others were celebrating Independence Day. Her vision blurred as fireworks began to explode and brilliantly lit up the night sky.

Chapter Twenty

Owen knew he had been too glib with Rose. He had felt guilty the night of the ball in October for enjoying himself so much. He still felt twinges of remorse to have been having fun while Amanda had been struggling through her last days of life. He wasn't sure if he could forgive himself. He didn't know if Rose could.

The next morning, he waited and waited for Rose. He had assumed she would arrive early so they could discuss things. He eventually donned his suit coat and picked up Hope so she could go down with him.

They were walking toward the door when a loud rap interrupted his cloudy thoughts.

"Rose," he said in relief as he opened it.

He was astonished to see Gwen standing there with

a sheepish grin. He opened his mouth to speak, but so many questions tumbled around in his mind, he couldn't think what to say.

"I saw Rose leave the ball last night, and she asked me to come and help you out today. I see you're uncertain about what's going on."

"Yes, I . . ."

She let herself in. She seemed concerned. "She didn't explain anything to me, but she looked mighty upset by the time I saw her. She was having a run-in with Richard when I came across her, but I don't think that was the only reason she was distraught." She raised her eyebrows as if expecting some clarification.

"Dobbs? What was he doing?" His protective urges were rising.

"He had her by the arm. I couldn't hear them, but I could tell she was trying to get away."

He cursed under his breath. "Did he hurt her?"

"I don't think so. I think she was rattled, but I had the impression it was because of you."

"Yes," he admitted. "She discovered something about me that she couldn't face." He shook his head. "I was hoping we would talk about it today."

"Maybe she'll show up yet."

"I hope so." He exhaled. "I must go, let me tell you about Hope's typical day."

Every time the bell over the door rang, Owen looked up hoping it would be Rose. By the time he was trudging up the stairs at the end of the day, he was thoroughly disheartened. He didn't know what to do.

When he entered his home, Gwen got up off the floor where she was playing with Hope. Her hair was a riot and falling from its pins. Her white shirtwaist had a suspicious green stain on it. She was rumpled and seemed somewhat frazzled, but surprisingly in good spirits.

"Owen. I don't know how you or Rose do this all day." She pushed a wisp of hair out of her face. "I adore Hope, but I don't think I could do this again. You're going to have to go talk with Rose."

"I thought she would come to me when she was ready."

"I'll stay tonight as long as it takes," she urged.

"I don't know . . ."

"Go, go." She pushed him out. "Do it for your happiness and hers." The door slammed behind him.

He still wasn't so sure, but his feet carried him forward. He walked out of the store, but went east instead of west. He didn't know where he was going, but he needed to think.

Before long, he came to the House of Lords saloon on the southeast corner of Main and Broadway. Maybe he needed a shot of liquid courage. He entered the dim interior which smelled of smoke and liquor. He sat at the bar, ordered a beer, paid the barkeep, and took it in hand. He remained as he was for some time, staring at the froth as the bubbles slowly popped and disappeared in the amber beverage.

"Thought I saw you come in here," Logan drawled as he took a seat next to him.

"I thought I'd quench my thirst." He glanced at his still full glass.

"Looks like it," he joked.

Silence stretched between them.

"So what's turned you into a drinkin' man?" Logan asked.

"Rose."

"A woman. I should've guessed." He nodded wisely. "Did you two hit a rough patch?"

"Yeah." He wiped a stream of condensation that trickled down the glass with his thumb.

"Are you goin' to fight for her?"

He was taken aback by the question. "Rose is too good for me," he muttered.

"No one is perfect, man. I learned that the hard way and almost lost Ada when we were courtin'."

He shook his head. "I did something in the past. I don't know if she'll forgive me."

"You need to ask her. She's that kind of soul," he encouraged.

"Maybe."

"Think about it. She's worth the effort." He stood to leave. "Besides, you can believe if I didn't think you were good enough for her, I'd be talkin' to that other fella." He inclined his head toward Richard Dobbs who was downing a shot of whiskey at a corner table near the door.

"Thanks."

Logan hesitated thoughtfully and then said, "Bein' loved by the woman you love is the most amazin' thing. A man would be a fool to pass that up."

Logan left him alone to reflect on his advice. He knew he was many things, but he never wanted to be a fool. He stood, left his drink untouched, and headed outside.

Before he could exit the building, Dobbs hailed him. He was leaning back in his chair with his arms crossed.

"Couldn't help but notice you and your lady love were having problems last evening." He sneered.

"It's no concern of yours," Owen said curtly.

"Oh, but it is, my friend. Because, you see, if she's dissatisfied with you then I'll have the opportunity to get back in her good graces."

"That's not going to happen." He clenched his jaw.

"No woman has resisted my charms yet."

"You'll leave her alone," he ground out.

"We'll see, my friend." Dobbs gave him a haughty smirk.

"She made her choice when she told you to leave her alone." He turned and stormed out.

If he had any reservations about talking to Rose, they were gone now. He would go to her as quickly as he could get there.

The heat of the day was oppressive, but Rose couldn't stand to be under her mother's questioning gaze a moment longer. She didn't want to relate to her what had happened the previous night. She knew the excuse she'd given her for not going to work had been a flimsy one, and she was afraid her mother wouldn't hold her tongue for much longer.

She settled into the shade under the rose arbor. The flowers were almost spent from the summer heat. A breeze stirred the air enough to make it bearable.

She groaned inwardly when she heard the screen door squeak open. She wished her mother would leave her alone for a few minutes. She was shocked to see Owen coming out of her home. He placed his hat on one of the wicker chairs before making his way to her.

"I don't think your mother wanted to let me in." He gave her a small smile. "Do you want me to go?"

"No." She peered up at him. "Stay."

"First, I want to apologize. I knew when I was dancing with you at the ball in October that it was a dangerous thing to do. I have no excuses except that I enjoyed your company, but be assured that was the end of my interest then. I respected Amanda and our marriage. I wouldn't have ever done anything to damage that."

"Wait—"

"Let me finish, please," he hurried on. "You should know too how guilty I felt later. When Amanda died I couldn't believe how selfish I had been."

"Owen, I—"

"That said, I hope all that can remain in the past."

"Owen." She stood and placed a finger on his lips to stop him. "Let me speak."

Now that she had his attention she wasn't sure where to begin. She took both of his hands and held them tightly, willing herself to continue. "I *was* shocked at first, but I was embarrassed, also. To think I fairly threw myself at your feet without even knowing if you were married or not was humiliating."

"Ah, Rose."

"I'm sorry too. I'm sorry for running away last night and for making such a spectacle."

He leaned forward and kissed her tenderly. It was such a simple gesture, yet one that stirred her soul.

He pulled away slowly. "It looks like we both need to think first and react second."

"Yes." She chuckled.

"And let's promise to always talk things through no matter how difficult. I haven't had that kind of relationship before."

She nodded and snuggled into his outstretched arms. He smelled of wool, aftershave, and oddly pipe smoke. She savored the security she felt as his sturdy arms embraced her.

"I feel strong when I'm with you, Rose," he murmured into her hair. "Like I could conquer the world. It's a new experience for me."

She reluctantly stepped back so she could examine his handsome face. "I feel the same. I used to be so timid, but I feel courageous now. I know that if anything bad comes my way, I'll be able to overcome it."

"Exactly."

"Rose," her mother beckoned as she leaned out of the screen door. "Supper is ready, my dear. Owen, you may join us if you like."

"Thank you, Mrs. Dennis, but I need to get home," he called out to her mother. He turned back to her and said with a grin, "I need to rescue Gwen. She's been with Hope all day."

She giggled. "I'm sure she's ready to go home by now." She squeezed his forearm quickly. "Good-bye. I'll see you tomorrow."

He nodded, went to grab his hat, and whistled as he sauntered out the side gate.

Her mother emerged from the house. She definitely did not look pleased. "I assume he was the reason for your mood today?"

"Well, yes, we had a disagreement last night. But, all is well now."

"So I could see. You cannot carry on like that for prying eyes. What will the neighbors think?"

"I'm sorry. I thought we were secluded enough."

"This does not bode well for your employment situation." She crossed her arms.

"Mother, please—"

"Has he asked for your hand yet?"

She was surprised by the turn in questions. "No," she said.

"He'd better soon or I will not allow you to work for him anymore."

"But, Mother, I can't *make* him propose."

"There are ways to encourage a man that aren't of the flesh."

"Mother. I am not going to talk him into marrying me. He will ask if and when he is ready."

She marched off, knowing her mother was staring at her back. She had won this battle, but she also knew the war wasn't over until she was married.

Chapter Twenty-one

Rose succeeded for the next couple of weeks to keep her mother placated. She tried to show her they were the essence of propriety. Owen began walking her home in the evenings, pushing Hope along in her baby carriage, and they would all spend some evenings together in the parlor.

They apparently gained her mother's trust because she actually urged them one night to go to an ice cream social in Woodland Park and offered to watch Hope. They took her suggestion and left before she could change her mind.

Rose was relieved when they finally rounded the corner out of sight of the house. It would be so nice to be able to speak freely with Owen without other ears listening.

"Whew." She exhaled loudly. "I was beginning to think she'd never have faith in us again."

"She didn't?" he asked with alarm in his voice. "Why in the world wouldn't she?"

"Oh, she saw us being . . . amorous . . . that night when we reconciled," she paused. "She has threatened to make me quit working for you."

"What?" He stopped in his tracks.

"She thinks it's improper and dangerous to spend so much time alone together."

"Why didn't you tell me? I had no idea." He sounded worried. "You reassured her that we would never do anything unbecoming, didn't you?"

"Of course."

"I don't know what I'd do if you couldn't watch Hope. She adores you. I do too, for that matter. I enjoy the thought of you only being a few steps away all day." He gave her an affectionate smile.

"I like it also." She put her arm through his, and they began to stroll again. "So, we'll behave and not give her any reasons to bring up the subject again."

"Yes."

When they arrived at the park, Rose was plenty warm from their excursion. Tables were set up and decorated with bunting. They were served homemade ice cream and cake. They took their bowls of sweets to a nearby bench.

"This is delicious," he commented.

"Mmm. If this doesn't cool us down, nothing will," she said as she savored a bite of vanilla ice cream.

"You don't even look a bit uncomfortable."

"Why, sir, I'm fairly wiltin'," she said in her best Southern belle accent. She batted her eyelashes.

He let out a surprised laugh, almost spitting out a bite of cake. "My little Rose will surely bloom again after this refreshment," he drawled.

She giggled. She hardly ever joked or acted silly. It was so fun to not feel she had to be reserved around a man.

As they were finishing the last morsel, Owen pointed with his spoon to a spot on the north side of the library where it was apparent work was in progress. "I heard that's where a fancy fountain is going in. It's supposed to have three tiers and be over seven feet tall. It's going to have a circle drive around it and curve around to Bell Street."

"That will be grand."

"We'll have to come see it when it's finished."

She felt a little thrill about him speaking of a future together. Even if it was something as simple as walking to the park, it still made her feel aglow with affection.

The cadence of a marching band could be heard coming up the street. The group of colorfully uniformed men turned as a unit into the park and marched to the bandstand area.

"Could we listen for a while?" Rose asked.

"Of course we could."

They deposited their bowls and spoons before making their way to the group of seats surrounding the bandstand. The small band was rather accomplished and played several different styles of songs. Rose thoroughly enjoyed herself. She loved watching people who had mastery over their instruments. At some point, she noticed out of the corner of her eye that Owen wasn't watching the performance but her.

"You are so lovely," he said quietly.

She was at a loss for words. She didn't know how she could verbalize how handsome he was or how kind or how honest. Everything seemed so insufficient. "Thank you," she said softly.

He took her hand in his and slowly rubbed his thumb along the back of her knuckles. They sat that way until after the band finished playing, packed up, and left. The last man in the audience removed himself from the area as the fireflies began to show themselves in the twilight.

She leaned back in her seat, lifted her face to the darkening sky. She peered through the canopy of the trees at the stars that were beginning to emerge. She used to feel small and alone when she watched the stars, but no more. She felt so tall it seemed she could reach out and touch them.

"What are you thinking about?" he asked.

She diverted her gaze to him. "Nothing. Everything." She smiled. "I only dreamed of a man like you. Now, here we are and you're mine," she whispered. She hoped she didn't sound too forward, but she had to tell him.

"And you are mine."

He kissed her cheek, then her lips. She returned it wholeheartedly and placed her hands on his face. They broke apart, but her hand remained. She caressed the stubble on his solid jaw. It was a curious mixture of rough and soft. His gaze was intense. Blood rushed through her ears and raced through her veins. She had never felt so alive.

She gave him a final peck on the mouth before disrupting their intimate moment. "We should probably go."

"Yes," he agreed. He took a deep breath as if to clear his senses. He stood and helped her to her feet. "It is getting late." He grinned. "I'm sure your mother is wondering about us, and I need to go milk Nan. She's probably miserable by now."

"Poor Nan." She smiled back. "I'd hate to think we tortured the poor animal, but I wouldn't have traded a second of tonight."

"Me neither." He put her arm through his, and they went off to the dimly lit streets.

A couple of days later, Logan walked into the store. "Hey, there," he greeted Owen.

"How are you today?"

"Fine. Just fine." He came up to the counter. "I need a couple of things for Ada."

"What can I help you with?"

"An old friend from her actin' troupe sent a letter, and she found my old supplies lackin'. First, the nib of the pen was bent so I'll need a box of those. Then, the bottle of black ink was all dried up. She also looked at my wrinkled stationery with a gimlet eye, so I'll take a box of some kind of pretty paper."

Owen chuckled, and found the items that Logan needed. He tallied the order, took his money, and began to wrap it all up. Logan leaned forward and looked over both shoulders before speaking. "I also needed to tell you somethin' I found out about Dobbs."

"What?" He had his interest immediately.

"He had told Rose he was goin' to buy old man Benson's house. He told me a while later that Benson backed out. Well, I saw Benson this mornin' and just happened to ask him about it. He told me that his house wasn't for sale and never had been."

"Really?" He somehow wasn't surprised.

"I knew there was somethin' I didn't like about Dobbs. Apparently, we can't trust the man."

"No, we can't," he agreed.

"I don't know how we can keep an eye on him, but we'll need to do it."

"Yes. I've been escorting Rose home at night. I'll continue to do so."

"I would if I was you." Logan nodded as he picked up his package. "I'd better go, Ada will be wonderin' where I disappeared to."

Owen didn't spend long at Rose's that evening. He wanted to stop by and see Gwen on his way home. He pushed the baby carriage up the sidewalk to Gwen's boardinghouse. He parked by the front porch steps, lifted Hope out, and knocked on the front door.

Momentarily, a middle-aged woman, Mrs. Brown he supposed, opened the door.

"Can I help ya?" she asked.

"I need to see Gwen Sanders," he replied.

"Surely. You can wait in the parlor. I'll go get her." She pointed to the blue room at the right, and she plodded up the stairs.

The parlor was simply decorated with a sofa, a couple of upholstered chairs, and a faded Oriental rug. He stood there waiting until he heard footsteps charging down the stairs.

"I knew it had to be you," Gwen said as she entered the room. "You're the only comely young man with a darling baby that I know." She touched Hope's cheek. "To what do I owe this wonderful visit?"

"It's not because of anything fun, I'm afraid. Logan and I have found out a couple of unsavory things about Richard Dobbs. I was wondering if you could use your pull at the newspaper to investigate his past."

She chuckled. "I don't know how important I am as the society reporter, but I'll try," she paused. "You know, I think he said he lived in Guthrie awhile. Next time I go back there I'll talk to a few friends."

"I'd appreciate it. If we can't find any more negative things, maybe I won't worry about him as much."

"I think you're right to pursue it. I didn't like the

hold he had on her that night." She put her hands on her hips.

He nodded. He tried not to get angry all over again at the thought of Dobbs' hands on Rose. "Like I said, I'd appreciate it."

"You're welcome. We want to take care of our Rose."

Every protective urge in his body was raised. He wanted nothing more than to keep her safe. "Yes," he agreed. "I do."

Chapter Twenty-two

The last Friday in July was an exciting day for St. Benedict's parish. Bids had been previously accepted for the brickwork, carpentry work, and for the installation of the slate roof for the new church. The foundation was set and the large cornerstone was laid and work was ready to begin. But, first, they would have a day of celebration.

Bishop Meerschaert was coming from Guthrie so the ladies of the church had been busy cooking cakes, pies, and other delectable items. The choir was prepared and arrived early in the morning to practice on the lawn next to the building site one last time.

When they were finished warming up their voices, Rose, Gwen, and Ada went to take a peek at the stone before the ceremony while Luke went to fetch Rose's mother. On one side of the cornerstone the Benedictine medal was carved along with the year, on the other side was *Soli Deo In Honorem.*

"To the honor of God alone," Gwen translated. She grabbed Rose's hand and then Ada's. "We are witnessing history in the making, girls. This new building will stand for hundreds of years. Our grandchildren's children will be able to go here."

Rose wanted to preserve this moment in time. Seeing it all unfold with her best friends was something she would always hold dear.

They turned away, and walked arm in arm.

Ada was the first to speak. "Will Owen be able to attend today?" she asked.

"Yes. Bob and Betty are closing the store for a few hours. They should all be here before long." It had been less than fourteen hours since she had seen him last, yet she could hardly wait until he would come.

"I think someone's in love," Gwen teased.

"How can you tell?" Rose grinned.

"Oh, I don't know." Gwen tapped her chin with her forefinger. "Maybe it's the telltale glow when you speak his name or the way your eyes constantly search for him."

She giggled. "Then I must be in love."

"I knew it!" Gwen said triumphantly.

"How wonderful!" Ada squeezed her arm. "Does he return the sentiments?"

"I think so. We haven't said it in so many words but—"

"But, when you know, you *know*," Ada completed.

She nodded with a smile.

Gwen looked at one and then the other thoughtfully. "So, you never have doubts?"

"No," Rose answered.

"There may be times when I get so mad at Luke I'd like him to sleep in the barn, but, no, I never doubt our love for one another." She grinned.

"Hmm."

"Do you have doubts about Walter?" Ada asked.

"No, no. Of course I don't." She flapped her hand, and peered off in the distance. "Isn't that Owen and Hope?"

"It is," Rose said enthusiastically.

Owen was coming from the south, pushing Hope in the baby carriage. He caught sight of them and waved.

Rose left her friends and met him halfway. "How are the two of you this beautiful morning?" she asked.

"We're wonderful," he said cheerfully. He reached out and squeezed her hand momentarily.

Hope squealed and held her chubby little hands out to Rose. She picked her up and kissed her cheek. "Are you ready to see Gwen and Ada?" she asked the baby who babbled back. "Well, then, let's go."

Owen stood in the great crowd that consisted of parishioners and other townspeople. He was so proud of Rose and the chorus. They were in complete harmony and sounded fantastic. Of course, he could pick Rose's clear, perfect voice out of the mix.

As they finished their hymn, Bishop Meerschaert, a large man from the French-speaking part of Belgium, stepped up to the cornerstone with the assistance of Father Schneider and Father Goin. He blessed the stone, the building site, and the congregation, and then after a few words he completed the ceremony and made his way through the throng. The choir began their final song and the crowd began to mingle.

As Owen's gaze followed the bishop, he noticed Dobbs on the outskirts leaning idly against a wagon bed. Dobbs seemed oblivious to the goings on around him. His eyes were fixed on Rose as she sang. It was obvious, even at a distance, that he was leering at her.

Owen put a foot forward, wanting to wipe that look off of Dobbs' face, but he was holding Hope. He couldn't, he knew, but he sure wanted to. He resolved even further to watch over Rose and keep her from harm.

Later that evening, Gwen came over for a visit. After visiting with her mother for a while, Rose was finally able to get Gwen up to her room so they could chat.

They plopped onto her bed which protested with a loud squeak. Rose leaned over and picked up a magazine off the nightstand.

"Have you seen this newest issue?"

"No."

Rose spread it across their laps and flipped the pages. "It has the latest illustrations of gowns from New York and Paris. There is even an article about wedding attire. Look at this gown."

She placed her finger next to an extravagant white dress bedecked with tucks, pleats, lace, leg-o'-mutton sleeves, and a long flounced skirt.

"My goodness. Isn't that a beauty?" Gwen gave a low whistle. "I like white wedding gowns, don't you?"

"I always imagined myself in a pristine white one, but I must be getting practical in my old age." Her lips turned up. "I think a pretty dress that can be worn again is a good idea."

"I agree. You can always fancy one up and wear a nice veil."

"Yes. Did I ever tell you I bought some lace for a veil?"

"You did? Is there an announcement I should know about?" Gwen grinned.

"No." She chuckled. "I saw this when I worked at the store. It was so perfect, I couldn't resist." She went to the large barrel-topped trunk at the foot of her bed. She opened it and pulled out the yards of folded white netting. It spilled from her hands and exposed the openwork scalloped edging with embroidery around the leaf and flower designs.

"Oh, Rose." She fingered the fine, soft material. "It's perfect. You'll be a radiant bride."

"You'll probably be hearing those wedding bells before I will. You're already engaged."

"That's true."

"Have you and Walter set the date yet?" she asked as she returned the veiling to the trunk.

"No. I still want to write that novel." She sighed. "I realized after the day I watched Hope that it'll be next to impossible to write it after I have a family."

"It wouldn't be easy. You would have to snatch moments when you could." She nodded. "Have you started writing it?"

"Oh, I've tried several times. I'll come up with an idea, but when I start to put pen to paper it sounds silly," she paused. "You know, it's not even so much that I want it to be published. I just want it to be good."

"It will be. Just don't give up."

"I wish I was as positive as you are."

"You aren't? You've always seemed the picture of confidence to me." She was truly astonished.

"I must be a better actress that Ada," she joked, but her expression soon turned serious. "No, I'm usually pretty sure of myself, but I do worry about a few things."

"Like what?"

"My writing is one. I just feel compelled to do it, but I'm afraid I won't be able to." She seemed unsure whether to continue. "Walter is the other."

"Really?" She was concerned for her friend.

"I don't think I've actually voiced it to myself, but . . . I've seen both you and Ada fall in love and it just doesn't seem that I feel the same way about Walter."

"You don't love Walter?"

"I do love him." She held up her hands in defense. "I just haven't had all those giddy feelings that girls seem to have . . ."

Rose held Gwen's hand.

"I've assumed that kind of passion will come when we're married. I'm not so sure now."

"I'm no expert, to be sure, but every match would be different, wouldn't it? Wouldn't the personalities of the couple make a difference?"

"I would think so. Dear Walter isn't the most animated soul I've ever met, yet he has such fine qualities." Gwen gave her a quick hug. "Thank you, Rose. I feel more courageous already. When I go back to Guthrie for a visit in a couple of weeks, I will be able to appreciate all the positive things about him and not dwell on any negatives." She seemed to have regained her cheerfulness.

"Yes," she agreed, but secretly she hoped she had given sound advice.

Gwen rubbed her hands together. "Now, let's look at those wedding dresses again."

Chapter Twenty-three

One evening, after a couple of weeks had passed, Rose and her mother were sitting on the back porch. They were enjoying some tea while waiting to see if the dark clouds would bring any moisture.

A clap of thunder sounded in the distance, and Aletha hurried out of her house carrying a large basket. She began taking her wash off of the line.

"I was wondering about something," Rose began.

"Yes?" Her mother raised her eyebrows.

"They're having a book shower for the library tomorrow night. I'd like to go, but Gwen is in Guthrie and Owen has some book work to catch up on. I was wondering if you would watch Aletha's children so I could ask her to go with me."

"That's a splendid idea. She works so hard. It would be a nice diversion for her," she agreed.

"I'll ask her." She rose and went to the fence.

Aletha spotted her and came over. Rose extended the invitation along with the offer for child care.

"It sounds nice, Rose, but I don't have anything nice enough to wear to a function like that." She wearily brushed a wisp of hair out of her face.

"We're about the same size. Why don't you come over a little early tomorrow and we'll find something for you. I have plenty of mourning clothes to choose from."

"I couldn't impose."

"It's no imposition. My friends and I do it all the time." She knew it was a slight exaggeration, but she hoped to convince her.

"Well . . . it does sound fun."

"Then you'll go?"

"Yes." She smiled slowly.

"Come about seven. I should be ready by then."

"That sounds fine."

Thunder rolled again and a few large drops began to fall.

"Better get the laundry in." Aletha waved and went back to her work.

Promptly on time, there was a knock at the door. Rose opened it and found Aletha with children in tow. The girls were peeking out from behind her while she held the baby with one hand and little Henry's wrist with the other.

"I saw your fella leave, so I thought we'd come on over," Aletha said.

"You're right on time." She motioned them in.

Her mother appeared with a ready smile. "How are my favorite neighbors?" she greeted them. She took Willie from his mother and said, "Don't you look fine, Willie?" She caught Aletha's eye. "He only has the faintest flat scar on his chin."

"Yes, ma'am. I don't think he'll be bothered by it when he grows up."

"No, indeed." She captured Henry's hand and asked the children. "I was just about to eat supper. Would you like to join me?"

The girls nodded and Henry jumped up and down. She led them to the kitchen as Rose and Aletha went upstairs.

She led her to her room where she had laid out several outfits across her bed for Aletha to choose from. She had already freshened up by putting on a white shirtwaist that was covered with Cambric embroidery with a gray gored skirt.

"How fine these are." Aletha fingered the material on a few of the waists. "I believe I'll wear my own skirt." She glanced down at her serviceable black skirt. "I've gotten too thin since my husband passed. Your skirts probably wouldn't fit. I've had to take this one up a bit."

She gazed at the clothes again and went immediately

to a dove gray shirtwaist with black lace around the high collar, yoke, and cuffs. "This one is lovely."

"Try it on," Rose encouraged. She turned her back to give her privacy.

After several moments of rustling noises, Aletha asked, "How does it look?"

It was a little too big on her slight frame, but the renewed vigor in her countenance made her beautiful.

"Perfect," she replied.

They went down, put on their hats, picked up two books, and grabbed a couple of umbrellas as it appeared rain was threatening to fall for a second evening. After farewells were said, they walked to the Carnegie Library.

The tall, tan bricked building had four marble columns out front and a domed roof. It had opened the previous year and was a handsome addition to the town. They entered, deposited their umbrellas by the door, signed the register, and donated their books to help build the library's supply of volumes. The interior was decorated with cut flowers, ferns, and palms that were arranged artfully throughout the various rooms. There was a table set up in a corner covered with a red damask table cloth. A huge cut-glass punch bowl was in the center.

"How does some punch sound?" Rose asked.

"Good." She nodded.

As they each picked up a cup of punch, strains of a violin echoed through the building. Rose followed the sound as she made her way past the women and men who were socializing. Aletha was close on her heals as they found the room where the music was emanating.

She recognized Miss McMannus, a local talent, as she began to sing. They crept in and found seats so they could enjoy the entertainment. Miss McMannus performed several fine solos. She was followed by a Mrs. Rowe who was as equally gifted.

After the applause abated, Aletha twisted in her chair. "I've had a wonderful evening, Rose. It's been so nice to have some time to myself, but I need to get back. I miss the little rascals." She smiled. She didn't seem as weary as she did the evening before.

"I'm glad you could come with me. I think I'll go too. But, I'd like to stop by and see Owen for a few minutes before going home."

She gave her what looked like a sly grin. "I'll let you see your fella alone. I'll go on by myself."

They arose, retrieved their umbrellas, and made their way to the street.

"Looks like we'd better hurry. It's starting to sprinkle." Aletha opened her umbrella.

Rose followed suit and said, "Tell Mother I'll be along shortly."

She waved and went south on Broadway while Aletha hurried north. Rose turned right on Main. She was damp around the edges by the time she made her way down the alley to the mercantile.

She unlocked the door and was surprised to find Bob and Betty going through crates.

"Good evening, Rose," Betty greeted with a pencil and paper in her hand.

"You're working late," Rose commented, hoping it didn't look too forward to be coming over at night.

"Yes. Bob decided we needed to do an inventory of our stock. We're not ones to stop until we finish something."

"I was on my way home from the library book fair and I thought I'd drop by for a minute or two," she said.

"He's up there." Betty nodded toward the upstairs.

She hurried up. She knocked lightly on Owen's door, knowing that Hope would be asleep.

He looked astonished when he saw her. "I wasn't expecting to see you again tonight. How nice this is." He left the door ajar as he stepped onto the landing. He was still wearing the brown trousers from his suit, but was relaxing with the collar unbuttoned on his white shirt.

"I couldn't resist coming by for a few minutes." She grinned.

"Did you have fun?"

"Yes. We had a nice time. There was music and singing."

"I'm glad you had a good time."

He held out his hands, and she snuggled into his arms. She ran her fingers lightly along his strong back. She had the wicked thought of wanting to pull his suspenders off his shoulders.

She let out a sigh infused with a chuckle. "I'd better go. Mother won't like that I come over this late and Bob and Betty are probably wondering what I'm up to."

"You're right," he agreed, but didn't loosen his hold.

He gave her a quick kiss. She reluctantly moved out of his grasp. They went down the stairs together.

He opened the door and said, "Be careful. I'll see you tomorrow."

"Good-bye." She gave him a final smile, raised her umbrella to fend off the falling rain, and went out into the dark night.

Owen had just locked the door when the telephone rang. He answered it, wondering who would be calling at this time of night.

"Owen? Is that you?" Gwen asked.

"Yes."

"I found out some information about Richard Dobbs from a reporter friend here in Guthrie." Even through the static, her voice sounded concerned.

"What is it?"

"Apparently, he roughed up a saloon girl. He broke her arm and nose, but because of her profession no charges were filed. But, he was *encouraged* to leave town."

"No." His heart dropped to his feet.

"I'm afraid so. He's not someone who should be around Rose."

"I've got to go. She's walking home by herself."

He hung up. He turned to Betty. "I just found out something terrible about that fellow who used to court Rose. Can you listen for Hope while I walk Rose home?"

"Of course I can."

He started up the stairs to get his hat and dress coat. But, before he was halfway up, the telephone rang again.

"Gwen. I don't have time," he muttered. He clattered back down and yanked it off the hook.

"Hello. Owen?" Mrs. Dennis asked. Her voice was shaky. "Is Rose still there?"

She sounded really upset. He hoped she wasn't too angry. He wanted to placate her as soon as possible. "No, ma'am. I—"

"Oh, no! Owen you must find her."

"I was just about to—"

"You don't understand," she said urgently. "Aletha was just attacked. Right outside. She was able to make it to my house. She said the man grabbed her from behind and began to beat her before he realized who she was. Owen, he thought she was Rose!"

"I'll find her." He left the receiver dangling as he ran out the door.

His heart raced. Every bone in his body was prepared to protect Rose. Mrs. Dennis didn't say who the perpetrator was, but he knew. It had to be Dobbs. He emerged from the alley and looked in both directions before running toward Rose's house. He was breathing hard, but he was trying to listen intently to his surroundings.

He passed two buildings, and then came to a vacant lot. An umbrella and a woman's hat were lying in a puddle on the sidewalk. He heard the muffled oaths before his eyes could find two shapes in the shadows. He knew even before he could see their features that it was Dobbs and Rose. He had her mouth covered with his hand, and she was kicking with all her might.

Before he could react, Dobbs threw her against the building and slapped her so hard her head bounced off the bricks. Owen would never forget the sickening sound of that blow against her flesh.

"Nooo!" he roared. It was such a guttural, primeval sound that he didn't recognize his own voice.

He bolted toward them. He slipped once on the wet grass, giving Dobbs time to turn around. He scrambled to his feet and stayed low so that his shoulder smashed into Dobbs' midriff. They crashed to the ground. He got off two good punches to Dobbs' sneering face before three men pulled him off.

Two of them held onto Dobbs while the other tried to restrain Owen.

"Whoa, there," the tall, skinny man who was holding onto him said.

"We were at the Rock Island yards over yonder when we saw what was happening," one man explained.

The skinny one released him. "I'll go fetch the police if you can stop from killing the man."

Owen nodded. Fury was beginning to drain from him as he hastened to Rose. She was in a crumpled heap in the rust-colored mud. He sank next to her and took her in his arms. Her head rolled to one side. Blood was streaming out of her nose and dripping onto her white shirtwaist.

"Rose. Rose!" He patted her cheeks with grimy fingers.

Rain splattered her eyelids and face. The metallic odor of blood mingling with the smell of clean water would forever stay with him.

"Rose, speak to me," he urged.

Her eyes finally fluttered open. She was dazed at first, but at length was able to focus on him.

"Owen?" she mumbled.

"You're safe now," he said tenderly. He looked over his shoulder at the men who were waiting. "Take him to the police, give them your statements about what you witnessed, and tell them we'll make our complaints as soon as she's able," he instructed. "If they need us any sooner, we'll be at B & B Mercantile. I'm getting her inside."

He gathered her in his arms and stood as the other men went on their way. He held Rose against his chest. She desperately clung to him as he hurried for home.

Chapter Twenty-four

Rose was not really any burden to carry, but Owen's arms were aching by the time he burst into the stockroom.

"Rose has been hurt. Call her mother," he ordered Betty before heading upstairs. He gently laid Rose on his sofa.

"We'll ruin it," she whispered.

"It's just furniture, it'll clean."

He glanced at Hope to see that she was still sleeping peacefully. He then hurried to the lavatory and found a fresh white towel. He dampened it with cool water and went back to Rose. He dropped to his knees next to her.

Under the soft light of the kerosene lamp, he gently dabbed the blood from under her nose. She winced, but didn't shy away as he tended to her. Her lower lip was beginning to swell and there was a small split where blood had already congealed. An angry red mark covered her left cheek and the purple-blue beginning of a bruise was appearing.

She took the towel from his hand and held it to her nose to staunch the trickle.

Betty poked her head into the room, and he went over to her. "Mrs. Dennis will be here as soon as possible and she will bring Dr. Maxwell with her since he was finishing his examination of Mrs. Cornwall. Do you need me to help with anything?"

"No. Not right now," he told her.

She left and he turned back around. Rose was so pale. She lay deathly still. He couldn't breathe until he saw her chest rising and falling.

What would he do if Rose was taken from him too? He couldn't let his mind think about that. What scared him the most was that she should die without her knowing how much he loved her.

"Rose?"

She opened her eyes and gave him the faintest of smiles. She began to shiver, and she could no longer hold the towel. Luckily, the flow of blood was drying.

"I wish I could get you in some dry clothes," he muttered.

"I'm . . . I'm not cold," she said as her teeth rattled.

"I'll get a blanket." He retrieved the folded quilt at the end of his bed and wrapped it around her.

"H-h-hold me."

He picked her up, sat down, and cradled her in his

arms. He pushed wet strands of hair away from her face. He caressed her uninjured cheek. He wanted to heal her, to take away her pain, but most of all he wanted to love her for the rest of her life. Her trembling finally subsided.

"Rose?" he spoke softly.

She gazed up at him.

"Rose. I love you."

Tears welled up in her big blue eyes.

"I'm sorry. I shouldn't have told you now. You've been through too much tonight."

She raised herself up and her eyes searched his. "I love you too, Owen."

"If something worse had happened to you—"

"But it didn't. I'll be fine." She tried to be brave, but a faraway, panicked look filled her eyes. "If you hadn't saved me when you did, I don't know what he would have done to me."

"But I did," he said gruffly, hoping to bring her back to the present and not to that terrible moment.

A soft rap came at the door.

"I wish I could stay in your arms forever." She sighed.

"I do too." He kissed her temple. He got up, deposited her onto the sofa, and went to open the door.

Mrs. Dennis rushed past him. An older man followed. He was apparently Dr. Maxwell. Betty stayed in the background with him.

"What happened, Rose? Are you hurt badly?" Mrs. Dennis asked as she made room for Dr. Maxwell by Rose's side.

"I don't think I'm hurt that much."

Owen turned on the electric light so the doctor could see properly. He could hardly believe that Hope stayed asleep. The doctor put his fingers on either side of Rose's nose.

She cringed slightly before continuing. "It was raining, and I had my umbrella up. I didn't hear Richard come up behind me. Before I knew what was happening, he was towing me away. He . . . he slapped me, and I hit my head on a brick wall."

Dr. Maxwell continued his examination by looking at her eyes and feeling the back of her head.

"Is that the extent of your injuries?" the doctor asked.

She nodded.

"Well, you're one lucky young lady. Your nose isn't broken, and you don't appear to have a concussion. There is a nice-size lump on the back of your head, and you'll be black and blue for a week or two, but I believe you'll mend just fine."

Owen exhaled at the news.

"Aletha wasn't so fortunate," Mrs. Dennis said.

"Aletha?" Rose was shocked.

"Richard mistook her for you. He pulled her arm out of its socket and bruised her ribs. Dr. Maxwell attended to her needs just before we came here."

"I knew he was no good," Rose said forcefully. "Where is he now?"

"In jail," Owen said. "Some men took him there. We'll go talk to the police tomorrow when you're up to it."

Rose slowly put the blanket aside. She assessed her soiled skirt and ruined, blood-stained shirtwaist. She stood with aid from Dr. Maxwell. She swayed for a moment, and then held her head high.

"We'll go now. I want them to see what he did to me."

"Oh, darling, are you positive?" Mrs. Dennis took her hand.

"Yes."

"Then the three of us will go." She placed Rose's hand into his. "We need to ensure that he never does this again."

Going to the police station and telling her story again made for an extremely long night. It was after midnight by the time Rose and her mother finally arrived home. Aletha and her children were sleeping on pallets in the parlor.

Rose was physically and emotionally exhausted as she and her mother climbed the stairs. They went directly to the bathroom. Her mother helped her out of her destroyed clothes. Rose stood in her chemise and corset. She tried to take the remaining pins out of her bedraggled hair with trembling fingers.

Her mother turned on the faucets and helped her kneel by the bathtub. She washed her hair for her like she had done for her as a child. Her hair had to be washed twice before all the mud and filth was rinsed away and the water ran clear down the drain.

Her mother then filled the tub for her and left her alone. When Rose finally sank down into the warm water, her thoughts ran back to her ordeal. She saw it over and over in her mind's eye. Just as she was about to give in to the terror of it all, she made herself remember that she was safe.

She forced her mind to turn from the terrible things that had happened that night and remembered how it felt to be encompassed by Owen's arms. Most important was the fact that he loved her. To know it without any doubts was a wondrous thing.

She smiled at the thought, and was abruptly brought back to reality by the pain in her face.

"I'll heal," she told herself as she gingerly touched her sore, throbbing face. "I *will* heal."

Improve, she did. With every day that passed, the aching that filled her body and mind lessened. The nightmares that plagued her at first became fewer so that she was eventually able to rest at night.

She stayed within the confines of her house for an entire week. Owen and Hope came every evening. Ada and Luke visited as soon as they heard, and Gwen dropped in as soon as she made it back into town.

One afternoon, Rose sat on the front porch with some embroidery. An older buggy pulled up in front of Aletha's house. A tall, thin man jumped down and hurried around. He helped Aletha to the ground. Aletha's arm was still in a sling, and she walked stiffly.

Rose waved to her, and she came over as the man began to unload a large trunk.

"How are you?" Rose asked.

"I'm on the mend."

"Do you have relatives staying with you?"

"No." She glanced over her shoulder. "John Posey and I got married today."

"You did? I didn't know you were seeing anyone." She was taken aback.

"We belong to the same church. He's a widower with two older girls. We got on just fine," she said matter-of-factly. "He asked me to marry him a month or so ago, but I couldn't see myself forgetting William yet." She rubbed her forehead. "When I was . . . attacked . . . last week, I realized I didn't want to be alone anymore. John's a good man. His girls will be a help to me. So, I took him up on his offer."

"Do you love him?" she blurted without thinking.

"Sometimes a body doesn't have time to wait for love. I had it once; maybe it'll come along again." She gave her a small, resigned smile.

"Are you coming in, Mrs. Posey?" Mr. Posey asked from Aletha's porch.

She turned to go.

"Congratulations," Rose offered.

"Thank you," Aletha acknowledged before going to join her new husband.

As Rose returned to her needle and thread, she wanted to weep. She found it awfully sad that anyone should marry out of convenience. To bind your life to someone you didn't love seemed to be a wretched existence. She thanked God that wasn't her lot in life.

Owen took the ring out of the case. He turned the cool metal around in his fingers and watched the gems sparkle. He was positive this was the one Rose liked.

He put it in his vest pocket. He walked to the cash register. He wrote the sale in the ledger, entered it in the register, and put the money in the till. The purchase was complete.

He didn't know how or when he would propose to Rose, but he knew it would be soon. He didn't want to spend any more time than necessary without her as his wife.

Chapter Twenty-five

Rose was invited to Bob and Betty's for lunch after church on Sunday. She wore a linen dress of the palest pink that was sprigged with tiny mauve flowers and green leaves. Her new straw hat was decorated with pink silk flowers and a white satin ribbon. Her bruise had faded into a slight yellowish color, but all in all her injury didn't look too bad.

She arrived at the large white house that had burgundy trim just before one o'clock. Owen admitted her into the entry hall and gave her a loving smile. A wide, elegant staircase led up to the second floor. He ushered her across the newly varnished wood floors, through the finely decorated parlor that had an ornate oak fireplace mantel, and into a spacious dining room with tall oak wainscoting. A row of four tall windows looked out into the enormous backyard with two pecan trees.

"There you are, Rose." Betty smiled as she placed a platter of fried pork chops on the table along the side dishes of corn on the cob, string beans, and baked apples. "We're ready."

Bob helped Betty into her chair while Owen assisted Rose. Hope was playing with a ball happily under the windows.

They ate a nice meal, but Rose thought it seemed to be at a rather quick pace. She had just put the last bite of apple in her mouth when Betty stood up and began to clear the table.

"I'll put these in the kitchen for now and finish cleaning up later. It's such a nice day; I believe Bob and I will take the little mite for a walk." She disappeared with her last load. When she returned, she picked up Hope. "Why don't the two of you enjoy yourselves on the back porch?"

"Oh . . . um . . . yes. That would be nice," Rose agreed. Betty seemed to be behaving oddly, but Rose dismissed it as the room cleared and Owen led her to the rear porch.

The porch was at least thirty feet long and a generous twelve feet wide. The ornate railings and fret work were painted white and dark red to match the trim on the house. The floor was painted a handsome shade of green and the bead board on the ceiling was a pale blue.

The area was spruced up with potted palms and hanging ferns.

"Bob and Betty's entire house is lovely, but I believe this is the most perfect spot," she said as she admired her surroundings.

He took her hand and led her to the far end that held a large white wicker table and a set of four wicker chairs. In the center of the table was a phonograph machine with black and brass amplifying horn and oak case with fluting and Gothic pillars at the corners. A large music disc was on the top.

"These are so expensive. I've only seen one at a time or two up close."

"Bob bought it for Betty on their last anniversary. Would you like to hear it?"

"Of course I would." She clasped her hands under her chin in anticipation.

He turned the handle on the side to wind it and the disc began to spin. An orchestral rendition of a Viennese-style waltz by Rosas called "Over the Waves" began playing. The sound was scratchy and wasn't perfect, but it was amazing to hear.

Owen bowed like a proper gentleman. "Miss Dennis, I thoroughly regret not having the pleasure of your company on the dance floor at the last ball. Could I entice you to join me now?"

"Of course, fine sir." She grinned, placed her hand in his, and they danced around the porch. She so enjoyed being in his arms. "I love this song. When I was a child, I saw Mr. Rosas conduct a band at the World's Columbian Exposition in Chicago. I had to buy the sheet music even though it was more popular for the violin. I had a friend whose mother used to play it for me on hers."

"I had no idea." He seemed amazed. "I listened to several that Betty had, but when I heard this one, I knew it was the one."

The song ended, and they came to a stop. She was breathless, but not only from the physical exertion. He continued to hold her in his arms. Neither of them seemed to want to move away.

"I love you," she whispered, hoping to hear it from him again.

He was still for the longest moment. He placed her hand on his chest. "There. It started beating again. To hear you say those words makes my heart stop." He brought her hand to his lips and kissed it. "Ever since my parents died, I've closed off my heart. I thought I was being strong by not fully loving someone, but instead I wasn't fully *living*. I tried to ignore your gentleness, your beauty, your gracefulness . . ." His mouth trailed from her cheek to her temple.

He suddenly stepped back, smiled, and threw up his hands as if to concede defeat. "I surrender. I surrender to love and to loving you."

He dug into his vest pocket, dropped to one knee,

and as he looked up at her he said, "I love you, Rose, with my entire heart." He placed the ring she had admired at the store on her finger. "Will you marry me?"

She yanked him to his feet. "Yes, yes, yes!"

She smothered him with kisses and almost knocked them both over. He caught her, twirled her around, and set her down with her back against a porch post. He pressed against her, his hands entwined through her hair and his lips moved along her neck. It sent a shiver up her spine.

"I can't wait until you're my wife," he murmured against her skin.

An intense yearning radiated from him as she clung to his shoulders. The passion she felt for him was unlike anything she had ever experienced. "I don't want to wait either, Owen. I don't want a long engagement."

His smoldering eyes studied hers. "Do I dare hope? Are my nights alone soon to be over?"

"Yes."

He shook his head as if to clear it. "When?"

"What about on Hope's birthday at the end of October?"

"Less than two months?" He grinned. "I think I'll survive that long. But . . . Hope's birthday is on Sunday this year. Why don't we marry the day before? You're the only mother she has known; let's make it official before she turns a year old."

"That's a wonderful idea!" she exclaimed. "Now, let's

go tell my mother. She'll be delighted." She grabbed his hand, and they raced around the house like children.

As Owen and Rose emerged from the side yard they caught sight of Bob and Betty pushing Hope along the sidewalk in front of their house. They hurried to them, hand in hand.

"She said yes," Owen informed them. His grin relayed only some of the happiness he felt.

"Best wishes!" Betty hugged them both. "So our plan worked?" she asked him.

Rose giggled. "You were part of the conspiracy, I take it?"

"Yes. He told me what he wanted to do and I tried to help."

"Congratulations, my boy." Bob pumped his hand. "Now that's all settled, Betty and I have a proposition for you." He glanced at Betty who nodded in approval. "Ever since you joined us, we've been toyin' with the idea of expandin'."

"Expanding? How?" he asked.

"We want to open another store in Oklahoma City," Betty said.

"Does that mean you're going to close the one here?"

"Oh, no, my boy. We want to make you partners," Bob informed him proudly. "You'll run the store here."

"Partners?" He was awestruck. It had always been a dream of his to own a business.

Betty said, "Yes. And since we'll be moving to the city, we'll need to sell this house and we think Hope should have a big yard to run and play in—"

"What she's tryin' to say is that we'd like to sell you the house, and at a fair price, I might add." Bob stroked his mustache.

"No . . . I can't believe it." He was getting choked up. What a marvelous day. "I can not fathom that I am soon to have a family of my own, a business, and a home."

"If it's agreeable to you both." Betty smiled.

He looked at Rose. Her countenance showed restrained excitement as she nodded.

"It's a deal." He shook Bob's hand again and hugged Betty. "Thank you."

He grasped the handle of the baby carriage. "Now, I have one more task to perform today," he told Betty. "I need to talk to Rose's mother."

The weather was pleasant as Owen, Rose, and Hope walked the five blocks to Rose's house. Hope seemed to be enjoying her ride as the breeze blew in her face. She gnawed on her fist and slobbers covered her face as she tilted her head up to them.

"Rose is going to be your mama. Isn't that wonderful, Buttercup?"

Hope removed her hand long enough to babble her approval, and then returned to her business.

Rose smiled at him, and placed her hand on his as he continued to push the buggy.

"You don't know how happy you've made me," he

commented. His heart was so full he thought it might burst.

"I feel the same, Owen. I've loved you so long. I feared you would never notice me."

"Oh, I noticed you, all right. I just wouldn't let myself give in to my feelings for you." He looked into her eyes and felt secure from seeing the adoration returned.

Before they knew it, their little journey was over. Rose picked Hope up and carried her as they entered her house.

"Mother. Owen and I have returned."

"I'm in here, my dear," Mrs. Dennis said from the parlor.

They found her sitting by the empty fireplace embroidering some white fabric. She placed it aside on a small table next to her chair.

"How are you today, Owen?" she asked politely.

"I'm good. No, I'm wonderful." He grinned nervously. "My day will be complete once I ask a favor of you."

"What would that be?"

"I would like your blessing to marry Rose."

"Of course you may." A slow smile crossed her face as she picked up her sewing again. "I was hoping you would ask."

She held up what looked like a linen piano scarf. She had embroidered green vines along the entire edge. At the end, in the center, her needle was sticking into the material. She was finishing the rose-colored design. At closer inspection he saw the initials *R* and *O* intertwined.

"Oh, Mother. Thank you."

"You may not be able to get your piano up the stairs in your apartment, but it's yours whenever you have a house to put it in," Mrs. Dennis offered.

"Actually, ma'am, we're buying Bob and Betty's house. If it all works out, we'll start our married life there."

"That is wonderful news." She stood and gave him a motherly embrace. "I'll be proud to call you my son and Hope my granddaughter."

He wondered how many times in one day a man could be so close to tears. "Thank you." The simple words seemed inadequate to express his gratitude and hope for the future.

Chapter Twenty-six

The end of summer continued to be an unusually wet season. In spite of the rain, work continued on the church. Rose made frequent trips by the site to see the timbers rise in the air.

When Rose told Ada about her engagement to Owen, Ada seemed almost as excited as she was. Ada insisted that she hand-sew a wedding dress for her. She wouldn't take no for an answer, and Rose finally gave her an enthusiastic and appreciative yes.

Toward the end of September, Ada and Gwen planned to spend a Saturday helping with wedding preparations. Ada needed Rose to do a final fitting on the dress before adding all of the embellishments.

Before Gwen arrived, Rose tried on the gown in her room. She admired Ada's handiwork in the mirror. The white silk draped across her perfectly. It had the modern puffed sleeves and high-necked collar. There were many careful tucks in the loose bodice. The slim skirt was encompassed by a wide ribbon that fit around her waistline. It was tied in a simple bow at the rear and two long ribbons flowed down to the short train.

"It's lovely," Rose breathed.

Ada turned around and came to her. She began to button the long row of covered white buttons up the back of the gown.

"I wanted your suggestions before I continued with it," Ada said. "I thought I would sew on some lace and put some swags of pearls across the front of the skirt."

"Hmm . . ." She studied her form. "Now that I have it on, I love the simplicity of it. Why don't you only put a little lace on the collar, sleeves, and yoke? Nothing else."

Ada peered around Rose's shoulder and admired the reflection in the mirror. "I agree. Fluid and graceful. Just like you."

She moved in front of her and tugged here and there. "The shoulders are fine. The length is good. I might shorten the sleeve a tad. What do you think?"

"Yes. A bit. Otherwise, it fits like a glove." She shook her head. "I can't believe you've finished this so quickly."

"Well, you know I love to sew, and I had to be fast when our troupe was on the road. Besides, it keeps me busy. I don't like to be idle."

A knock came at the door as it opened. "Are you decent?" Gwen grinned as she entered.

"As decent as I can be," Rose replied with a smile.

"Oh, Rose, you're just beautiful," Gwen gushed as she clasped her hands. "I'm so happy for you."

"Thank you." It was the most wonderful feeling in the world to have her friends share her joy.

They made a fuss over her and draped the veiling on her head to visualize the best way to prepare it. They decided that attaching it to a few hidden combs had the most pleasing effect.

Gwen began to fold the veil. "I hate to put a damper on things, but I was wondering if you two had read the accounts in the newspaper about the train wreck?"

Rose nodded sadly.

Ada said, "No, I haven't seen a paper in a while. What happened?"

"West of Guthrie, a Rock Island train from Texas was headed north between Kingfisher and Dover when a bridge collapsed and it went into the Cimarron River."

Ada gasped. "Your father wasn't on board was he?"

"Thankfully, no. He works for the Santa Fe."

"How many casualties were there?" Ada asked.

"At first the reports were exaggerated. They think about eight to ten now. The engine and the first few cars fell in." She visibly shivered. "I can't imagine the terror they felt, especially the women and children, as they fell into the flood waters."

"Oh, I agree," Rose said.

"They had a list of the injured passengers today. One of them was a name I recognized. If it's the same person, Josh Flynn, he was a great friend when I was a girl. We moved away and lost track of him and his family. I haven't been able to find out if he survived his injuries or not."

"How terrible," Ada remarked.

"It is. I hadn't thought of him in years." Her eyes held a faraway look as she reminisced. "We were such pals. We were devastated when my parents wanted to move. He promised to find me some day to marry me."

"That's so sweet," Rose said as she squeezed her shoulders to comfort her.

"It was. For years, I would look up the road from my window to watch for him. I couldn't tell you when I finally let that go."

"Most of the time we grow out of our girlish fantasies," Ada said.

"You're right." Gwen gave them an unconvincing smile. She fingered the material of Rose's dress. "But, sometimes our dreams can come true."

By the time autumn arrived, so did the trial of Richard Dobbs. Rose dreaded the entire process, but Owen was there with her every moment. Along with them, Aletha and the three railroad workers gave their testimonies.

Richard appeared aloof most of the time, but as the jury quickly came back with the verdict of guilty for two counts of assault his eyes flashed with hatred and indignation. He was sentenced to thirteen years in the merciless Kansas Penitentiary.

"They're just women!" he had shouted over his shoulder to the twelve men on the jury as they led him out.

The crowd present had gasped at his outburst, and she had been trembling as Owen had led her away. She was so relieved that was over. Now, she could focus on her new life that was about to begin.

In the weeks before the wedding, Bob and Betty found a suitable building for a store in Oklahoma City and a nice home nearby. They packed and moved things a little at a time.

A couple of days before the nuptials, Bob helped Owen move in his meager belongings. They had kindheartedly let him keep the secondhand furnishings from his apartment. His possessions were sparse, but it was all his. He and Hope spent the night in their new home. When Rose became his bride, his family would be complete.

The next evening, Rose and her mother arrived at her soon-to-be house with baskets full of items that she had saved for years in her hope chest. It seemed strange to her to enter without knocking.

"Owen?" she asked.

"We're in here," he said from the parlor.

They found them as Owen was placing his mother's vase on the mantel. Hope was crawling over to the sofa.

"We brought some linens and things," she told him.

"That's great. We're almost set." His gaze held hers for the merest moment, but the promises for the future gave her a thrill of excitement.

Her attention was diverted by Hope who pulled herself to a wobbly standing position by holding onto the edge of the sofa. She concentrated on the wooden floor, then took a tentative step forward. It led to another step and another until she lost balance and dropped to her bottom.

"She did it!" Rose exclaimed. She dropped her basket and rushed to Hope. "You did it, baby! You've been working on that this week, haven't you?" She picked her up and twirled around with her, kissing her cheeks. "And, you did it in our new house. How wonderful."

Hope squealed in delight and patted Rose's face with tiny hands. How she loved this baby. She had taken care of her for months and Hope was such a sweetheart.

"Mama is so proud of you," she whispered in Hope's ear. "Mama is so proud."

Rose's mother offered to rock Hope to sleep that night. Rose and Owen took the opportunity to have a moment alone on the back porch.

"I must send Betty a thank-you note for leaving these plants out here," she commented as they went to stand by the railing and looked out across the yard.

"She knew you would like them," he said. He stood behind her wrapping his arms around her.

The nearness of his body almost distracted her from the fact that it was dark out. She had assumed after Richard was sent away her nightmares would go away completely, but she still had them once or twice a week.

She quaked, now, just thinking about it.

"Are you cold?" he asked incredulously, for the night was cool, but by no means cold.

"No." She felt she should tell him. Maybe she wouldn't feel so alone and afraid. "I've never been fond of the dark, but since Richard . . . attacked me . . . I've had nightmares."

"You have?" He turned her around so they faced each other. He took her shaking hands in his.

"It's always pitch-black in my dreams. I feel Richard's hand covering my mouth . . . suffocating me. I struggle for breath and finally wake myself up gasping and tremoring with fear," she whispered.

"Rose. I'm so sorry. I wish I could take them away, but I think only time and God can do that." He lifted her chin with his forefinger so she would look him in the eyes. "I want you to know that after tonight, you'll never be alone again. I'll be there to hold you, to light up the darkness, to tell you you're safe. I'll be whatever you need me to be."

She searched his eyes and saw the strength that she didn't have at that moment. She was comforted to know he would help her through this. "I only need you."

His lips tenderly found hers.

"I hope you know how glad I am that you're going to

marry me," he mumbled against her lips. "I'm the happiest I've ever been in my life."

She pulled away, ever so slightly, and studied his features. He seemed so sincere. They had promised to always talk to each other about everything. There was one last thing that had been nagging her. "You are happy?"

"Yes, of course." His brow furrowed. "Why would you even ask?"

"Well . . . I . . ." There was no going back now. She just had to do it. "I'm embarrassed to ask, and I'll only do it this once, but I can't help to wonder. Were you as happy with Amanda? I need to know the truth."

She could tell he was surprised by her question and tried to gather his thoughts. She prepared herself for the honest answer she knew he would give.

He drew back and took a deep breath. "Amanda told me one night that she wanted to get married. We were both tired of being alone. I was smitten with her, and I thought we should. I tried to love her as well as I could, but . . ." He shrugged. "It wasn't until you came along that I realized how fully and deeply and ardently I could love someone. My love for you is like a fire that will never go out. I'm burning for you and only you."

She heard the passion is his voice and saw the expression in his eyes. She believed that she was truly cherished. She knew she would never be resentful of Amanda again.

She threw herself into his arms. He caught her, gathered her up, and kissed her with such longing it made her want to weep. She would never doubt his love for the rest of their lives.

The momentous day dawned cloudy and cool, but by midafternoon the skies were clear and the temperatures mild and pleasant.

Rose was ready. Absolutely ready. The preparations to her hair, veil, and dress were complete. She held the curtain aside on the window in her room for the last time. She saw Luke and Ada coming down the street in his buggy to pick her up. She let the curtain drop, grabbed her small bouquet of white hothouse roses, and went down the stairs.

After her mother had been assured Rose didn't need any more assistance, she had gone to the church to see if there were any last-minute things that needed to be done. So, as Rose walked through the still, quiet house she reminisced about the wonderful time she had there. She could still hear her father's booming voice as he asked her to play the piano again. She could imagine her mother's gentle demeanor as she smiled indulgently. There was a tinge of sorrow for the passing of her old life but, truthfully, she was so positive and so excited about beginning her new life that there was no room in her mind for sadness.

She gave the parlor, which seemed empty without the piano, one last glance before she went out the door. She lifted the train of her dress and hurried down the walkway.

Luke was waiting for her. He whistled. "You look like an angel."

"Thank you." She took his hand. He helped her up beside Ada in the rear seat.

"Yes. You are beyond beautiful," Ada agreed.

She smiled at her friend and held her hand as they drove off.

"Are you nervous?" Ada asked.

"No. Not at all."

"I wasn't either. When you're sure of your choice, there isn't anything to be scared of, is there?"

Rose grinned and shook her head. They were silent for a few moments. Ada was uncharacteristically fidgety. She seemed as if she was about to burst about something. Rose raised her eyebrow questioningly.

"You found me out." Ada laughed. "This is your day and I was going to wait."

"What is it?"

"Luke and I are going to have a baby sometime in May." She glowed.

"Oh, Ada, I'm so happy for you!" She hugged her.

"I'm almost afraid to say it out loud yet. It's so early. Things could happen."

"Try not to worry about that. Just revel in an answered prayer, as I am."

"Yes." Ada nodded. "Yes. We will."

It wasn't long before they pulled up in front of the church. Luke helped her down. Ada adjusted Rose's veil, kissed her cheek, and went ahead to find a seat.

Luke paused with his hand on the doorknob. "I wanted to tell you what an honor it is to walk you down the aisle."

"I couldn't think of anyone else I'd rather have. You've been a wonderful friend to me."

"I'm the one who's proud to call you friend." He nodded toward the door. "Are you ready?"

"Yes."

He opened it, and they waited in the tiny vestibule. Sister Mary Louise, who had been watching from the organ, began playing Wagner's "Bridal Chorus." The congregation stood.

Rose's eyes were drawn to her handsome Owen. He stood at the end of the center aisle in a new black suit and white bowtie. The expression on his face was a mixture of awe and joy.

She stepped forward. She could not wait a minute longer to become Owen's wife and Hope's mother. She savored the fact that her prayers and hopes had been answered as she went forward to be joined forever to her beloved.